AN ARMY OF LIES

AN ARMY OF LIES

THE FIRST ANGELO BARSOTTI NOVEL

RYAN SPELL

Ryan Spell, LLC
Lake St. Louis, MO

An Army of Lies
Copyright © 2023 by Ryan Spell
All rights reserved.

No part of this publication may be reproduced, distributed, or transmitted in any form or by any means, including photocopying, recording, or other electronic or mechanical methods, without the prior written permission of the publisher, except as permitted by U.S. copyright law. For permission requests, contact Ryan Spell, LLC, at www.ryanspell.com.

Published in the United States by Ryan Spell, LLC, Lake St. Louis, Missouri
First Edition

The story, all names, characters, and incidents portrayed in this production are fictitious. Any similarity to real persons, living or dead, places, buildings, and products is coincidental and not intended by the author.

Edited by Karen L. Tucker, CommaQueenEditing.com
Book design: Peggy Nehmen, n-kcreative.com
Cover knife image: pikisuperstar on Freepik

ISBN   979-8-9874618-0-8 (hard cover)
           979-8-9874618-1-5 (paperback)
           979-8-9874618-2-2 (ebook)

Library of Congress Control Number: 2022923466
BIASC
FIC022090 - FICTION / Mystery & Detective / Private Investigators
FIC022000 - FICTION / Mystery & Detective / General
FIC031010 - FICTION / Thrillers / Crime
FIC050000 - FICTION / Crime

I want to dedicate this book to my children,
Carson and Oliver, to become
whatever they truly want to be.
It's never too late to do what you want.

PROLOGUE

A BITTER WIND WAS knocking branches against the house as flurries fell, adding to the dusting of snow already on the ground. The second set of logs were crackling in the fireplace as she made coffee with a bit of Irish cream liqueur to calm her nerves. Her husband was due home soon, and she had a lot on her mind.

She carried two cups of hot coffee into the living room and set them on the table. She and her guest sat in silence before finally each reaching for their cups. Normally, conversation between the two was easy, but tonight was different. He could sense something was bothering her.

The night had begun like any other night they shared: cold drinks, always something strong, and straight into the bedroom. Usually, things proceeded slowly, and passionately, but tonight she seemed rushed, like she wanted to get it over with. This affair had been going on for just over two months, and tonight was the first time he felt that she was somewhere else, wanted to be anywhere else.

Finally, she broke the silence. "I'm telling my husband about us!"

He sat there stunned, unable to say anything. She said, "It's over! I cannot go on living like this."

Suddenly, he stood up, threw his coffee mug into the roaring fire and rushed into the kitchen. He began slamming cabinets and drawers. When she finally got the nerve to go into the kitchen, he was holding a knife. She screamed and ran toward the front door. But he was quicker. He grabbed her from behind and slit her throat.

As he stood over the body, he began to cry. He kept saying over and over, "He's my best friend, my best friend, my best friend..."

CHAPTER 1

IF YOU STEPPED INTO my apartment, you wouldn't describe it as a home or an office but a storage unit. Stacks of paper and binders cluttered every surface, and boxes spilled their contents onto the floor. But this was where the magic happens, where cases are solved…when I take them. I've had many cases over the years, but it has been slow lately. It's not like I haven't been getting calls, but I just haven't wanted to take on a lot. I was in a bit of a slump, and I wanted something that sparks my interest, a slump buster.

As I searched through the before-mentioned heaps of paper, I found what I was looking for. I reread the news article from two years ago that I've read a thousand times when I hear a soft knock on the door. I knew who it was because I asked him to come by and help me out. "One second. I'll be right there, Lewis."

I neatly tucked the newspaper clipping back into the binder. I take in the bare walls, save for a clock, mismatched furniture, and the mess everywhere as I walked to the door. I used to live in a completely clean and color-coordinated house. My wife had done all the decorating, purchased furniture, and created feng shui for our harmonized living space. It's not like that anymore.

There's a man at the door, but he wasn't Lewis. This man was tall and well-built. He wore a three-piece suit and tie, polished wingtip shoes, and didn't have a hair out of place. "Are you Angelo Barsotti?"

"I am. May I help you?"

"I hope so." Even his speech was perfect. *What could this guy want from an investigator like me?*

"I'm guessing you're here because I'm a private investigator. But I'm not taking any new cases right now." Why did I say that? I *needed* work. Sure, I paid the bills with my bartending job, but just barely. This work is what keeps me from needing to choose one meal a day instead of three.

"Look, just hear me out first. I'll tell you what I need, and then you can tell me yes or no. Please, I beg that you at least hear what I have to say, and I'm not one for begging. Have you seen any of the local murder stories on the internet or watched the news lately?"

I was old school, and I read the newspaper every day, hoping that one day I'll see what I'm looking for. But that's not why he's asking, so I simply said, "Yes."

"Then I'm sure you've read about the Helen Mazer murder. And that their main suspect is Craig Mazer, her husband. I've known Craig a long time, and he wouldn't have done this. He did *not* do this!" he shouted. "I know he didn't! I owe Craig my life, Mr. Barsotti, and the cops aren't looking at anyone but him. I need your help. Please, again, I ask you to look at his case."

As I stood there listening to this man, I kept wondering why he's here and not Mr. Mazer himself. Also, this man obviously had serious cash and could probably hire a team of high-priced investigators. Why me? So, I ask him, "If Mr. Mazer isn't guilty and needs my help, then why isn't he here? Why isn't he pleading his case to me? Why is he not talking to a lawyer, or the cops? Why does this fall to you? And what, exactly, do you want me to do about it?"

"Craig is still in jail with his lawyer, but he asked for my help. He's grieving and can't comprehend that they think he is the killer. I want you to find the actual person who murdered Helen."

"Look, Mister...?"

"Dogon, Grant Dogon."

"Look, Mr. Dogon, as I've stated, I'm not taking any new cases at this time. But I am expecting someone, and I must get back to what I was doing."

"Please, Mr. Barsotti, I know you understand what Craig is going through! He just lost his wife and is being blamed for it. I know that..." Grant hesitated, "that you lost your wife. That someone took her from you, and they still haven't found who did it. Wouldn't you want to know?"

So that's why he came to me. Of course, I wanted to know! I've been trying to figure that out for the last two years! Every day I agonized over what I could have missed. So yes, Mr. Dogon, I do want to know! But all I said was, "Yes, but I'm not taking any new cases. I'm sorry."

"I have money. I'll pay double what you normally charge. I'll pay whatever you ask."

I told him, "It's not about the money, Mr. Dogon. We're just not taking this on right now."

"OK, but if you change your mind..." he said as he handed me one of his cards. It was shiny and heavy, like a credit card.

I put the card in my pocket as he turned to make his exit, then Lewis walked in.

"Who was that? Do we have a new case? What can I do?"

Lewis is my best friend, has the best intentions, and is always ready to go. He grew up here in New York, just like me. Well, not *just* like me. He was and is very well off, never having to work a day in his life. We walked two very different paths to end up where we are today. Lewis Pollard was loyal, a little eccentric, and always willing to go the extra mile. He's what most people call a trust fund kid. He even had the look of a trust fund baby, with good looks and an air of confidence, but he has a heart of gold. His family has money and continues to make it. His family has been a part of the largest diamond company in the world, De Beers. He is well off.

"That was Grant Dogon, and no, we do not have a new case. Let's finish up what you came over here for."

"Grant Dogon? As in Dogon Tech? As in, one of the wealthiest people in the U.S., the world? Do you know that he was one of the first to mine crypto currency? What was he doing *here*?"

Lewis knows a lot. Usually, it's all about the latest fads or the hottest new product trends. I didn't pay much attention most of the time because I had enough useless information in my head already. But every now in then, he would catch me off guard on how much he *actually* knows about *everything*.

"He wanted help solving a murder case. Have you seen the news about the Helen Mazer murder?"

"Of course. Craig Mazer is the number two guy at Dogon Tech, Grant's right hand. It's been all over the internet how he murdered his wife."

"Well, Mr. Dogon says that Craig didn't do it, and he wants me to find out who did. I told him no, and that's that. Can we please get back to what you came over for?"

Lewis wanted to talk more, but like I said, he knew everything, including when to not push me further.

CHAPTER 2

AS THE DAY WENT ON, I couldn't help but to think about Craig Mazer, Helen Mazer, and Grant Dogon. I did not want to get involved in this case, but something Grant said got to me: *Wouldn't you want to know?*

Two years ago, my wife was murdered in our home. I was out on a case, and someone broke into our house. The police claimed it was a robbery gone wrong and that they probably didn't expect anyone to be home. But she was. They took everything from me that night. I haven't taken many cases since—partly because I blame myself for not being there, and partly because they still haven't found who did it. I've been pursuing my own investigation and moonlighting as a bartender at a friend's bar to pay the bills. I haven't found many leads, but I can't give up.

Lewis and I were wrapping up an investigation that we had done for a defense team that was trying to prove their client had not robbed a convenience store. We had found video surveillance that proved that they had the wrong guy. We just needed to finish putting together our files and the bill to send off for payment. I needed Lewis to take these things over to the defense team today so that we would be paid quickly. I was heading to work at the bar soon.

Lewis gathered all the necessary paperwork and headed out. I jumped on my computer and began researching Grant Dogon. I learned that he had started his first tech company when he was only twenty-three and fresh out of the military. He essentially made a better homing missile for the Department of Defense and then it sold for a lot of money. He went on to create a few other tech inventions and eventually to mining the first crypto currency. Lewis was right, but I hadn't doubted him.

I dug deeper into his military life and accolades. That's when I found the picture of his battalion and in it was Craig Mazer. Craig and Grant looked like an impossible pairing of friends. Grant was a square-jawed, well-built physical specimen, while Craig just wasn't. He was a little on the shorter side and had a puppy dog look to him. He was a little on the pudgier side with a hairline that was already receding when this picture had been taken. It was obvious even from the photo that Grant was the leader, the one everyone looked up to.

As I continued researching, it seemed that Grant never had any kind of love life. All the stories stated the same thing over and over, that he was too busy developing new things, and basically printing money, to ever sustain a relationship. And from the outside, it looked as if Craig had continued riding his coattails, moving on with Grant from company to company. The only other information I could find on Craig was about the murder.

I glanced up at the clock—6:15! I had lost myself in the stories and now was going to be late.

CHAPTER 3

I ARRIVED AT MCGINTY'S at 6:45 P.M., fifteen minutes late. I ran to the back room, looking for my boss and friend, Roy McGinty. I needed to apologize, but he wasn't back there. Then I heard, "Angelo! I didn't hire you for your good looks or because you're a great bartender, because you are neither! Now get out here so I don't have to do your job anymore!"

Roy was at the bar having a good laugh at my expense, but I guess I deserved it for being late. Luckily, he did hire me because we've been friends since the second grade when I helped him figure out who kept stealing the cookies from his lunch every day. Seems crazy, but I've always been investigating. Even crazier, it was our second-grade teacher Mr. Hambrel. Basically, we set up a stakeout of Roy's lunch bag, always with someone keeping watch. It worked out perfectly because the first day that we were watching, as the rest of the class went out for recess, we said that we needed to use the restroom then watched as Mr. Hambrel went through the lunch bag and took the cookies. We decided that instead of telling on him, we would set him up. The next day, we had made a special batch of cookies with laxatives. And after Mr. Hambrel spent the entire second half of the day in the restroom, he never touched Roy's cookies again!

We remained best friends all the way through high school. During college and adulthood, we remained close and kept in touch. When he opened a bar, he told me that it was a cop hangout. I asked if I could help out here and there, aiding me in my investigations as I chatted up the cops.

I jumped behind the bar and apologized, but Roy just laughed and said, "Get to work and grab me a beer." I did just that. I've worked at McGinty's for right under ten years now. I didn't always need the money, but I always needed the information. When cops drink, they get a little talkative, and I can usually get more information from them there than I could in a normal working relationship. So, as long as I was doing my job, Roy let me keep working there.

McGinty's was a typical dive bar. Dark lighting, pool table, dartboards, small wooden tables and chairs, and a lot of charm. Roy also has a wall of fallen policeman that he calls "Cheers to Service: Fallen, not Forgotten." Roy has a plaque made for any fallen cop that has ever been in the bar, even if they had moved on.

This night was like any other night at the bar, but all the conversations seemed to be about the Craig Mazer murder. Maybe they had been for a while, but tonight I paid more attention. They all believed they had their guy. No one in there thought any differently than that Craig had murdered his wife. They said he had motive but wouldn't tell me what it was and that he had no alibi. I tried to listen more closely, and serve more drinks, but I couldn't get any more answers.

About an hour before last call, in walks Grant Dogon. He didn't fit in here, and everyone took notice. He strolled right up to the bar and said, "So, Mr. Barsotti, have you changed your mind yet? I have money, like I said before. I can pay you whatever. Just say you'll take this case."

"Mr. Dogon…"

"Call me Grant."

"Fine, Grant, I'm working right now, so can I get you something to drink?"

"I'll take a scotch, double, neat."

As I made him the drink, I kept wondering why he was pushing me so hard, and why it was me that he wanted. Was it only because of my wife, that he thought he could get me to do it by pulling on those heart strings? Did everyone else already turn him down?

"Here you go. Can I get you anything else?"

He wasn't paying attention to me anymore; instead, he was listening to the same conversations I had been hearing all night—that they had their guy, and that guy was Craig. I could see in his face a mixture of sadness and rage. And I could tell he was about to do something that wasn't going to end well.

So, I snapped him out of it. "Yes, I'll take the case. But we can't talk here, and I think it would be best if you left right now. You can come by my office tomorrow, 10 A.M."

He didn't say a word, but he drained his drink in one gulp, lay a hundred-dollar bill on the bar, and strode out.

Roy came over after Grant left and asked if everything was OK. He said he had noticed things getting tense but knew I could handle it.

I told him, "Yeah, we're good, Roy. I just have a new case. Thanks for watching out for me, though."

CHAPTER 4

I **WOKE UP THE** next day with a pang in my chest. What had I agreed to? I didn't want this case. I didn't want to involve myself in the investigation of a murder when I already had one to figure out. But I had told Grant that I would, and if there's anything you should know about me, it's that I stick to my word.

It was early, but I called Lewis anyway. I told him I had taken Grant Dogon and Craig Mazer's case, and that I needed him over here as soon as possible to start gathering background information on all things Grant Dogon, Craig Mazer, and Helen Mazer.

While I was waiting for Lewis to arrive, I continued my research on the internet, but this time on Craig Mazer. There was little information out there. He appeared to be your everyday working man. But then I found a picture of Craig and Helen together. She was stunning. Again, Craig was not. Craig had worked for Grant since they left the military. He was not high up in any of the companies that Grant had started, apart from his present title, but he must have done well for himself from the sales of each company. Craig and Helen had an upscale home in Cobble Hill, which is a nice part of Brooklyn. Other than that, there wasn't much to say about Craig himself.

Craig and Helen had been married for twelve years. They had met soon after Craig had gotten out of the service and were married a year later. There was a big write-up about their engagement and upcoming nuptials in the newspaper during that time. Helen was a socialite and mainly could be spotted around town with her group of wealthy friends. Helen also had her own money as an Instagram influencer. She had a large following of her designer wardrobe and posted nearly every day. She had over 242,000 followers that amounted to approximately $10,000 per month from advertising sales. She had a face for the internet, with long brown hair and fair skin. She was beautiful in each of the outfits she posed in, and each outfit appeared to be made perfectly to fit her body. The couple seemed to be well off and were always photographed together at events. They had appeared to be happy. But that's only what the camera showed, and everyone knows we usually only put our best self out there online. I would ask Lewis to dig deeper into their real lives.

I started to clean up my desk a bit, organizing the stacks, so that I would at least give off an appearance of being put together. Even if I was a mess, I would not give off that impression. I moved boxes and picked up piles of papers and put them in their appropriate place. Now I looked like a hoarder, but at least an organized one. As I shut down the computer, a loud knock came from the door. I yelled to Lewis that it was open, and he bounced in through the doorway, clearly excited to get started. "It's just a case, Lewis."

"I know, but this is Grant Dogon, and he has serious cash. I may be wealthy, but compared to him, I'm slightly above middle class."

"Lewis, we'll treat this like any other case, with normal fees associated, and we'll work it like any other case."

"But—"

"No, Lewis, I know I need the money, but I'll do it the same way we've always done."

Lewis had tried plenty of times to give me money, but I always refused. I'd made it this far by doing it on my own. I know he's my friend and just trying to help, but I won't accept it. I could be a little hardheaded sometimes and pushed myself to the limits on how far I could stretch a dollar, but I liked the feeling of knowing I had made it on my own.

"OK, Angelo, but…" His voice trailed off as he decided not to finish his statement. Again, he knew me too well.

"Look, Grant will be here in a few minutes. I want you here for our initial interview. I want you to get a sense of him and why he's here and not using his resources elsewhere. Then, after he leaves, I want you to do a deep dive into Craig, Helen, and Grant. Not just what everyone else knows, but the actual details."

"Got it, Boss."

CHAPTER 5

AT PRECISELY 10 A.M., I led Grant to the chair across from Lewis and myself. Again, Grant wore an expensive suit, expensive shoes, and had the same perfect hair. I introduced him to Lewis and asked him to take a seat. Then I went over our investigation process. First, I explained what we expect from him, which includes open and honest communication about all things that can help in the case and an open door to people in his company. Then I told him what he should expect from us, which includes open dialogue and discovery of the facts. I said we would do everything we could to prove that Mr. Mazer was innocent, but if the facts lead us in the other direction, then we would let him know that as well.

He listened to everything without interruption until I went over the fee schedule. "Grant, we charge $200 per hour and need a $2,000 deposit to get things going."

At that point, Grant leaned over and set a briefcase on the table. "Here's $100,000 cash, and I have more if you need it. Just help me get Craig out of this."

"Grant, I can't take this. I'll charge you like any other client."

"Mr. Barsotti, I don't mean to insult you, but I have money and insist that you keep this. I won't take it back when I leave."

"Fine, but I'll give you a receipt for all charges and return your 'change.' Next, Grant, is that we need 100 percent honesty from you and Craig, like I said before. It will not help get us any further if you lie to us."

"Understood. So, where do we start?"

"Well, first we'll go over your account of what you know. Then we'll need to set up a meeting with Mr. Mazer's lawyer so that we can question Craig and get his story. So, Grant, what can you tell us? The police say that they have motive and no alibi, but you say that you know he is innocent. Tell me why."

"OK, I'm going to start off with some history first. Craig and I served together in the same platoon. That's where we met and have been pretty much inseparable since, and that was eighteen years ago. As you may or may not know, I have started and sold a lot of tech companies over the years, and Craig has always been with me. He wouldn't allow me to put him in charge or as an executive in any of my companies because he said he wanted to earn it. I respected that but always made sure that he had plenty of equity, so when we sold, he was well taken care of. And now, he's the vice president and chief operating officer of Dogon Tech, and he's earned every bit of those titles."

"That's a good start. Why don't you tell us about Craig and Helen. How did they meet? How was their relationship?"

"Well, as soon as we got out of the service, I started a tech company for the military, which I had planned on doing. And Craig met Helen soon after as well. They met at a service event for Wounded Vets, where they both were volunteering. Craig was there representing veterans, and Helen was the kind of person who loved to help people. Craig told me the next day that he was going to marry her. So, while I was going through the steps of starting the business, he was going through the stages of courtship. Helen was perfect for him. She accepted that he would work long hours helping me with the startup, and she would even bring us dinner, knowing that we hadn't stopped to eat. She was perfect for both of us; she believed in the company and helped in any way possible. The business was up and running for only six months when the military signed on to the homing missile system that I developed. Within two months, we sold the company for $22 million. I gave Craig 20 percent of the sale, and he took that and bought a house, a car, and a ring. She said yes, and they were married the following fall. As far as I knew, the relationship continued the way it started, like a perfect love story. Helen loved being with the other wives in the country clubs and even started her own fashion-inspired Instagram page that paid her well for advertisements. When Craig wasn't working, they would be out for dinners, Broadway shows, or whatever, but they would always be together. Sometimes, I would tag along. Nothing ever seemed different or off to me."

I cut him off at that point and asked, "Grant, can we get to the night of the murder. Why do the cops believe Mr. Mazer had motive? And why does he not have an alibi? Where was he?"

"From what the lawyer told me, Helen had sex before she was murdered, but there was no semen, so it was protected sex—meaning it probably wasn't with Craig. So, the prosecutor is saying that Craig got home from work and killed her. That he found out what she had been doing, whether she told him or he figured it out, and that is their motive. As for Craig's alibi, the coroner put the time of death between 8 P.M. and 10 P.M., but Craig says he didn't get home from work until 3:00 A.M."

"So, he does have an alibi?" Lewis questioned, a little too enthusiastically.

Grant replied, "Well, actually, he doesn't. We have a swipe card system to get in and out of the building, so it tracks the times a person goes in and out. It's how we can track billable hours for projects. But for that night in particular, the system was down—some internal error or a glitch in the system—and there were no recorded swipes the entire day. It affected the cameras as well—no recordings." As Grant became angrier, his voice rose. "This is all my fault! I wasn't there that night, and I should have been there to vouch for him. I should've fixed the system right away! This could all have been cleared up already!"

"Grant, I think that's enough for now. If you remember anything else, or anything that could help us, give me a call. I'll be in touch with you soon. Please set up that meeting with Mr. Mazer's lawyer so that we can hear directly from Craig what happened."

CHAPTER 6

AS I CLOSED THE door on Grant Dogon, I turned to Lewis. "What do you think?"

"I think that there's a briefcase full of cash here."

"Right, about that…I'd like you to take out the $2,000 for the retainer and take the rest to your place. It will be safer there than it will be in my apartment. Then I want you to start your digging. I need to know what's really going on here. There's something off, something he didn't tell us. He sure seemed angry and feels guilty about the security system shutdown."

"I agree something's not right with the whole story. What kind of tech company doesn't have a backup system? Mr. Dogon does seem to blame himself for the mess that Craig is in, but he definitely believes that Craig didn't do this. We need to figure out the alibi; that seems to be the main reason that Craig is in holding and being prosecuted for the murder."

"Lewis, do you already think Craig is innocent? Because I'm holding my opinion on that until we meet with him. I agree that Grant believes he's innocent, but that doesn't make it so. We must uncover all the facts and then draw our conclusions. We can't go into this with any preconceived outcomes."

■ ■ ■

I continued trying to figure out what Grant wasn't saying. He was convinced that Craig didn't kill Helen, but how does he know for sure? I needed to figure out where Grant was the night of the murder. I would need to approach that situation carefully, so that I didn't set off Grant. He seemed like a person I wouldn't want to be on the wrong side of. I also needed a list of people who knew the Mazers as well. If Craig didn't kill his wife, then who did, and why? I wanted to believe my clients, but everyone lies to help their own situation. Only the facts could lead me to the truth.

CHAPTER 7

I WANTED TO HAVE a look at the Mazers' neighborhood and house. I knew I wouldn't be able to get in because it was still a crime scene, but I wanted to get a feel for the place.

When I called Lewis, he said he'd send a car for me. He was still working on his research and asked if I could handle it alone. I told him that I'd put my big boy pants on and take care of it alone.

The Cobble Hill neighborhood in Brooklyn is lined with massive rowhouses built from a beautiful old brick design. The Mazers owned a duplex that they had renovated to make into a single home. The area is as suburban as it gets in the city. People were out walking the streets, kids played outside, and restaurants dotted the friendly neighborhood.

As I stroll past these brick homes, I noticed the yellow caution tape around a front door. This had to be the Mazers' place. Nicely manicured shrubbery bordered their home, with a dazzling picturesque design in stain glass was set in the front door. The brickwork of these homes always amazed me—how something so simple could be made into something so beautiful.

I decided to take a closer look and peeked through the window. It was very modern inside with high-end pieces everywhere. A dark brown and red stain seeped through the hardwood floor near the front door. As I was snooping around, someone tapped me on the shoulder.

"Excuse me, Mister, but you can't be here. There was a murder in that home."

I answered, "I know. I'm investigating the case." I turned to find an older gentleman who appeared to be in his mid-seventies.

"Are you a policeman? You don't look like a policeman."

"No, sir, I'm a private investigator. I'm working for Craig Mazer."

"Oh, I see. Well, I hope that you get Craig out of jail. He was a lovely man, and his wife was the best. There's no way he could have done this."

"Why do you say that?" I asked.

"I've known Craig and Helen since they moved in. I have lived in this neighborhood my whole life, and they were a great addition. Craig, when he wasn't working, was always helping people out around the community. He and Helen were always doing things for others. I don't think he could have done that to her."

"Well, I will take that into consideration. What was your name, sir?"

"Jenkins. Arthur Jenkins."

"Thank you, Mr. Jenkins, for your thoughts. I hope to do right by Mrs. Mazer."

"Me too. Nice meeting you."

CHAPTER 8

WHEN I STARTED WORKING my evening shift at the bar, I started paying special attention to a group of cops in the back. Roy said that they had been here all afternoon and were really "tying one on." I figured I would take a chance on my loose lips theory—that loose lips give tips—and buy them a round of shots.

I took the shots to the table, and they gave me loud and appreciative cheers. As I gathered the empty shot glasses, I asked them what they were celebrating.

"Just got finished with my first big case as a new detective! The DA said that he had enough to charge that asshole Craig Mazer with his wife's murder, so the guys are treating me to drinks! And I'm making sure I get *their* money's worth!" the youngish detective shared loudly with the entire bar.

"That's great news. Congrats! I heard about that case; it's all over the news. So, how did you catch the bastard?" I asked, trying to show I'm on his side.

"Poor guy, really; wife was cheating on him, and he killed her. Why can't these lowlifes just get a divorce? It would make our lives much easier!"

"Probably didn't want her taking half his money!" one of the other guys chimed in.

"And if you're going to lie about where you were, better make sure your security system is working! You'd think a tech guy would be better at tech!" another one yelled.

I tried to press the issue further. "What do you mean, his security system wasn't working?"

"Listen here, this guy said he was working when the murder happened, acted all upset about it, but we knew we had the right guy!" the younger one yelled, and they all gave each other high fives. "His company is the largest technology firm in the U.S., but there's no record of anyone working that night. Don't lie to us. We will get ya!"

"Well, nice work, guys. One more round on me, OK?"

In unison, they cheered and high-fived again. I felt that I had gotten as much as I was going to get. But I did confirm that some of the information from Grant was correct. I needed to talk to Craig to get his side. I needed to find out where he had been at the time of the murder, and if he was at work, what happened to the security system.

As I was cleaning up, the table of guys finally staggered out past me, thanking me again for the shots. But one of them stopped by the bar to say his thanks for the shots and give me a tip. Yet as soon as his buddies were out the door, he leaned in and said, "Look, I know who you are, and I know you're working on this case for Grant Dogon. He doesn't believe we have the right guy, and I actually have a slight feeling he may be right, but I can't do anything about it. So, if you happen to figure it out, or need anything, don't hesitate to call."

He handed me his card and walked out. He was the oldest of the group but seemed just shy of 50. He had salt-and-pepper hair and appeared to take care of himself. When he talked, the smoothness of his voice reminded me of a radio host. His card read "Detective Paul Tanner."

CHAPTER 9

THE NEXT MORNING, LEWIS and I got together first thing to compare notes. "First thing" to Lewis is 10 A.M., so I had plenty of time to go over all my online research, Grant's interview, and the detectives' comments at the bar last night. Also, around nine, Grant had called and said that we could meet with Craig Mazer and his lawyer at noon the next day.

I started by sharing with Lewis the events of the previous night and how they had matched up with what Grant had told us. I told him what I had found on Grant, Craig, and Helen, and he nodded along and then said, "Yeah, that's the internet stuff, but there's more."

As I waited for Lewis to go on, he just sat there. He liked to make me beg for his "professional sleuthing." Finally, I broke down, "Lewis, what do you have? I beg that you tell me so that I can laud you with congratulations and applause."

He broke into a big grin and started, "OK, we know about the military connection and that's how Grant and Craig met. They served all four years together on the same battalion. What Grant forgot to mention, though, is that he knew Helen long before he met Craig. They went to high school together, and Grant was the one to set them up. He knew they both were going to the event for wounded soldiers and apparently made some calls to make sure they would be working together. And from what I've gathered, Grant and Helen were never romantically involved, just good friends. Don't ask me how I know all this, but you know my sources are always good."

I have always wanted to know who or what Lewis's sources were because I could barely find a restaurant's address using multiple search engines. Yet within a couple of hours, Lewis could have the full report on the restaurant owners, their home address and phone number, and reservations for us with a limousine to take us there.

Lewis continued telling me how Grant had not lied about Craig's involvement in all the companies. Each one he would move up a rung on the corporate ladder but would always cash out big on the sale. At Dogon Tech, Craig was listed as the vice president and COO. He also found out that Dogon Tech is a private company but is supposed to go public next month.

"I'm not sure what they're going to do with the announcement of going public with the second-in-command being charged with murder. That doesn't help with high stock valuation," Lewis said matter-of-factly.

"No, it sure doesn't help. So, is this why Grant wants Craig to be innocent, or does he truly believe he didn't do it?"

"Well, that leads me into Craig and Helen's relationship. Apparently, since starting Dogon Tech, Craig has kept long and late hours. It also correlates with more and more posts from Helen's Instagram. Her posts weren't with friends at dinner parties or out on the town anymore. They were mainly posts of her showing clothing at home from brands that had given her things to try and promote. And from the information that I've gotten, it does sound like Helen had met someone else, and they'd been involved for the last couple of months or so. This is one of the loose ends I need to keep pulling on to get the full story, but that's where I'm at now."

We chewed on that for a while. It seemed that Grant's story matched some of the true story, and that some of the detectives' theories were also correct. It didn't mean that Craig did it, but we needed to get more answers to put it all together. I hoped the meeting with Craig the next day could help clear some of the picture up for us.

CHAPTER 10

IT WAS A FRIGID afternoon, and the rain was pelting the windshield at a steady pace as we pulled up to the jail. The building looked sad with the gray clouds and gloomy weather surrounding the decrepit concrete block walls. Craig was being held here until a court date was set. He had already been arraigned and charged, and he was denied bond due to him being a flight risk. When Lewis and I walked into the waiting area, Grant was there. He introduced us to Craig's lawyer Gerald Touré, pronounced *too-ray*. Mr. Touré was an older gentleman with graying hair and reading glasses. He looked like the typical lawyer you would see on TV or in a movie. He had a sense of pride in what he did and has seemingly been doing it for a long time.

Mr. Touré explained to us that we would be meeting with Craig with him, and all information would be protected under attorney-client privilege because we were hired as private investigators for the defense. He also told us that Grant would not be allowed to join us as he is not an attorney or an investigator. But Grant did have a message for Craig that Mr. Touré would give to him before we started. Grant had handwritten a note for Craig, which read:

*Hey soldier, hang in there. I'm here for you
and will help get you out, no matter the cost.*
–Grant

Grant left after reading the note one last time and patted Lewis and I on the back while saying, "Get our boy out of there."

They called us back to go see Craig. They took our cell phones and any other personal belongings. We were only allowed a notepad and a pen and the note for Craig after they thoroughly studied it. It was a long, windowless walk with walls that were bare concrete, the only color from water stains after years of neglect and decay. We were heading to the rooms reserved for attorney meetings. These special rooms had no cameras or listening devices.

When we entered the room, I immediately noticed Craig's appearance. The pictures on the internet seemed as if they'd been taken long ago, even though I knew I'd found more recent ones. This man had aged at least ten years since being in here. He had lost at least 15 pounds, and there was a frailty about him. We all gathered around the steel table bolted to the floor and sat in the cold metal chairs. Mr. Touré introduced us as we each shook hands with Craig. Then he handed the note to Craig. As Craig looked it over, it seemed to take forever as he read and reread the note, tears welling up in his eyes. We gave him a few minutes until he realized that we were all staring at him.

I broke the silence. "Craig, as I'm sure you know, Grant has hired us to investigate this case on your behalf. He tells us that you didn't do this, but we need to hear it from you and get your side of things."

"Mr. Barsotti, I could not and would not do this. I loved my wife. I still can't believe that she is gone." His voice was barely audible, and he had to catch his breath with every other word.

"Craig, I understand that you're very upset. I lost my wife two years ago, and I'm still dealing with it. But I'm going to ask you some tough questions, and I need you to be completely honest and as thorough as possible. Can we start with the night of the murder? We understand that you said you were working until 3 A.M. and came home to find your wife dead. What did you do next?"

"I called 911 immediately. I was crying and trying to tell them what had happened, and they kept asking me questions. I told them no, I didn't do it, I don't know who did it, and I didn't know if the person who did was still there. I got frustrated and hung up the phone. I knew they would come, and I wanted to sit there with my wife, just the two of us. Next thing I know, I'm being taken down to the station for questioning. Eventually they let me go, but I couldn't go home, so I went to a hotel. I sat in a hotel for two days just completely numb and cried."

"OK, thank you, Craig. I know this is hard. Can you tell us about your relationship with your wife? Were there any problems in your marriage?"

Craig gazed off into the distance before answering, "We had our problems like any married couple. But since starting Dogon Tech as VP and COO, I've been working a lot more than usual, and it put some strain into our normal lives. We had been having more petty arguments than usual, not going out with friends or by ourselves as much; basically, our time was compromised. You know that they told me my wife was sleeping with someone else and that's why I killed her?" He started crying but continued, "The cops continued to badger me about it, saying it over and over, trying to make me angry, but all I wanted was my wife back. I just want her! For her to be here!" Then he lost it completely, bawling into his hands.

"Craig, I get it. Lewis and I are going to step out and give you a few minutes."

Mr. Touré stepped out a few minutes later and asked if we could continue another day, that Mr. Mazer was unable to gain control of his emotions and would not be able to go on. I told him that would be fine but would need to happen very soon. He agreed and then stepped back into the room. A guard led us back to the front where we collected our things and left. We didn't expect to come out with so little information, but hopefully next time will be better.

CHAPTER 11

ON THE RIDE BACK to my apartment, Lewis and I recounted what Craig had said and how he had said it. He seemed very upset, and the feelings appeared to be genuine. But with us only getting partway through the interview, I was holding my opinion on innocence until we finish, but I was leaning that way for now. Lewis was on the same page as me, but he had that feeling again, the same one we had with Grant. Something was off, and we weren't being told everything. I told him that we were not done talking to Mr. Mazer, and we needed to see where the rest of the interview went before we dug too deep into the holes in his story.

Lewis had his driver drop me at my apartment. He said that he had an event to attend tonight but would be back to "finding the truth" in the morning—his words, not mine. Lewis likes to attend or throw as many events as possible. He is the most outgoing person I know.

I had a night off from the bar and was needing a break from this case. It had been a whirlwind of a few days, and if I grind too hard, then I lose myself and my priorities. I needed breaks in my life, and my breaks are taking quiet times to reflect on things, whereas Lewis uses his events and big dinners to get a break from things.

I decided to go to my favorite pizzeria, Mancini's Wood-fired Pizza. The owner is a friend of Roy's, so I know him well enough to go eat there and not feel like I'm eating alone. He treats me like I'm family, and his staff does as well. Every time I walk into the place, it's like I'm on a trip to Italy. The smells hit you and your journey begins. I always order three slices of different types of pizza, but I always get at least one slice of the Vodka pizza. It's to die for. It is a mix of pasta and pizza that comes together so beautifully in the wood-fired oven.

As I was starting on my second slice of pizza, in walked Grant Dogon. He looked right at me, and even as I was totally caught off guard and surprised to see him, I could tell he was expecting to see me there.

"Grant…" I mumble through a mouthful of pizza.

"Angelo, I've been looking for you."

"How did you find me?"

"First, I tried your place. Then I stopped by the bar, and the owner said you were off tonight and that I'd probably find you here if you weren't home. And he was right."

I would need to make sure Roy doesn't spoil any more nights off for me by telling people he doesn't even know where to find me. I guessed my "break" was over, so I asked Grant to have a seat. He ordered a slice then started right in on me, "What happened with Craig today? What do you have? How long until you get him out?"

"Grant, slow down. We didn't even finish the interview. Craig broke down part of the way through, and Mr. Touré said that we would need to continue another day."

"I want this mess over for me!" After a long pause, he added, "And for Craig's sake, of course."

But the pause was too long. I had caught that this was more about him than it was about Craig, even as he tried to save it.

He got up, asked for his pizza to go, and they handed him his box. As he headed toward the door, he looked at me, slightly embarrassed, but managed to say, "I know you're doing your best to get Craig out of this. I just want him to be OK." And then he left.

The owner came out and asked me if everything was OK. I told him that it was just a client, and he left it at that. I called Lewis and left a voice mail for him to meet me at my apartment first thing in the morning.

CHAPTER 12

I WOKE UP FEELING refreshed. It had been the mental break I was needing because I didn't spend any other time thinking about the case apart from when Grant interrupted my dinner. I took out the old newspaper clipping of my wife's murder, and I read the story again for the thousandth time. I always hang on the last few words in the article: "As of now, the police have no leads." And they still had nothing, same as me. I can't get over the fact that this is what I do for a living, and I can't even figure it out myself.

I often returned to that night, wondering if I had been home, would it have turned out the same? Would my wife still be gone? Would I be dead? Sometimes I think about how my life would be now if she were still here. Other times I think about how my small world would be affected if I weren't here. I always end up with the same thought—that I would trade my life for hers every time.

Lewis knocked on the door, interrupting my thoughts. Even his knock sounded cheery. Maybe he had something new, or maybe he just had a good time the night before. Either way, I called out, "It's open."

Lewis came in with a huge grin on his face. He said, "I met someone last night!"

"What's her name, Lewis?"

"Not a her, but a him."

"I'm sorry, Lewis, I didn't mean to assume, but I didn't know you went that way?"

Lewis broke into laughter and said, "No, I met someone that may be a lead in the case. Grant was at the event last night, and he spent a long time talking with this gentleman. I recognized him from the research I've been doing. His name is Jack Gaither, and he's right behind Craig in seniority at Dogon Tech."

"Wait, I saw Grant last night! He ambushed my dinner at Mancini's." Now that I thought about it, Grant did seem more dressed up than usual, but I guess in my shocked state, I hadn't wondered why.

"So that's where he disappeared off to! He left early from the event. What did he want?"

"He wanted details about how our interview with Craig went."

I recapped what I had told Grant. I also told Lewis how he had left me feeling that this was more about helping his company than it was about helping Craig. "So, what about this Gaither guy? Also, if Grant saw you there, why did he need to intrude on my dinner instead of just asking you?"

"Well, Grant never saw me. I didn't want to talk with him about the case until we had finished our interview with Craig, so I made sure he didn't see me. But when I saw him leave, I decided to talk to Mr. Gaither about Dogon Tech and the security issues. He knew who I was before I introduced myself and told me that Grant had told him to talk to us if we ever called upon him. He really only gave me the same information we've already heard and nothing else."

"Then what are you so happy about?"

"I got that feeling again. He was leaving things out, not giving me the actual story. It sounded almost word for word what we've heard about the security issues. Like it was part of a rehearsed script. There's something going on here, and it's more than this murder case! We have some work to do!"

CHAPTER 13

LEAVE IT TO LEWIS to be happy about more work, but he had a point. There definitely seems to be more going on surrounding Dogon Tech than just the murder. Grant gave me the impression that he's more involved than he's volunteering, and this whole mess somehow involves Dogon Tech and what effect it could have on the public offering.

Lewis and I discussed these feelings of mistrust, how everyone seems to have been told what to say, and how it could affect us getting Craig out of jail—if that's what he deserves. We needed to do a broader search and include Dogon Tech in it. Also, I let Lewis know that we were on to finish our interview with Craig at noon the next day. Mr. Touré had called that morning and said that Craig would be more prepared this time, so we would be able to wrap that part up. The only good part about not finishing up with Craig before was that we could now add a few questions about Dogon Tech and try to figure out what's going on there.

When it came time for lunch, Lewis said that he had some meetings to go to. Event planning or some board meeting, I'm sure. That was fine with me as I had to go over the questions for Craig and make sure that they were worded in a way that put him at ease, made him feel comfortable telling us what we needed to do our job. Lewis said that he would start a deep dive into Dogon Tech and its security through his sources while also continuing his checks on Craig, Helen, and Grant.

When Lewis was walking out, he noticed that I had left out the old newspaper clipping. He turned to look at me and said, "Don't worry, Boss, I'm still working all my sources on your wife's murder as well."

I gave him a hug, patted him on the back, and said, "Thanks."

As I shut the door, I broke down. I hadn't cried for a while, but today I did. I have a hard time being open with my feelings, especially in front of others. But for some reason, just knowing that someone else cared about my wife's case as much as I do meant a lot. I went back to my thoughts about how life would be if she could be here.

After an hour, I was able to pull myself together and get down to work. First, we needed to nail down what was going on with the security and see what Craig knows about it. Next, we needed to go through Craig's alibi and track down a way to prove it. Finally, we needed to figure out Grant's part in this and see if it's about him and Dogon Tech or about caring for Craig as a person and a friend.

Once I finished preparing all the questions for Craig, I got ready for work at the bar so that I wouldn't be late today. Lewis was going to meet me there. We do this thing during big cases when we need some help with information. I have Lewis come in and spend some money, spreading it around to everyone in the bar. It's another tactic in the loose lips theory. Everyone knew who Lewis and I are, but they liked the free drinks, so they talk, at least a little more than they would…and a lot more than they would if they were on the job.

CHAPTER 14

WHEN I WALKED INTO the bar, Lewis was already there and the drinks were flowing. I jumped behind the bar because Roy was sweating and needed a break. Lewis had kept him on his toes. Roy has put on some weight over the years, but spending most nights having drinks with customers will do that to you. When Lewis saw me, he jumped up and said, "Next round on Angelo!"

There were cheers all around. I started making our signature shot, the lava grenade. It's a deadly mix of tequila, spiced rum, and an energy drink. There were about thirty people in the bar, so the cozy bar was near capacity. Once I yelled "Shot time," everyone came up and grabbed one. When all the glasses had been taken and were being held high, Lewis stood on a chair and shouted, "To the boys in blue, we drink to you!"

Lewis was the outgoing one in our yin and yang relationship, as you may have noticed. I hold back and let things come to me. That's not to say that I don't put full effort into investigating, which was where I stood out. I liked all the little details that come together to fill in the puzzle. I liked figuring out each piece to see where it fits, and Lewis liked the puzzle as a whole. But this was why we worked.

Lewis and I met at one of his fancy galas. I had just finished a big case and was invited by the clients I had helped. I was standing alone in a corner, as I usually do at crowded events, when he approached me. He asked me who I was and who had invited me. He didn't say it in a mean way, just as a matter of curiosity. He told me this was his event and thought he knew everyone on the list. I told him who I was and why I was there. Once I let him know I was the investigator that broke the case for his dear friends, he had a ton of questions. He wanted to know everything that had led me to my conclusion and how I had gotten there. He was like a little kid with so much interest in every single word I spoke. We ended up talking about the entire case and how he had always wanted to help people, in a more personal way instead of with money only. We stayed in the event space four hours after the party ended. I told him that I probably could use an extra set of hands, and if he was willing, I would be willing to teach him. We figured out we had so much in common. He came to love my wife dearly, and even the silences we sometimes shared were special. Friends like that are hard to find. The rest, as they say, is history.

■ ■ ■

I was cleaning up the bar when Lewis came over to pay for the tab. He ended up buying everyone's drinks for the entire night. But he also had come away with some new information. He told me that the security system at Dogon Tech had been having shutdowns/glitches the past couple of months. They only lasted for about a day each time, so the night that Helen Mazer was murdered was another glitch day of many. The police hadn't figured out if these were done manually or were just that—a random glitch. Lewis also found out that the police always had Craig as their main suspect, but the police had two other people who were people of interest. He couldn't get any specifics or names from the cops, but it was one more lead for us to follow up on.

CHAPTER 15

AT NOON, LEWIS AND I were in the small cold waiting area again. At least we didn't have to run through the rain to get inside this time. We were looking around for Mr. Touré when we heard a female voice call out our names. When I turned to see who it was, I was speechless. This petite woman was a knockout. She was dressed professionally, but she had these sparkling blue eyes, a deep olive skin tone, and a smile that could make anyone smile along with her. She also had a small nose piercing that gave her a little extra flare. She also looked vaguely familiar, but I couldn't place her. I also noticed she wasn't wearing a wedding ring.

Lewis spoke up first. I'm not sure if he noticed my jaw on the floor or that's just who he is, but he said, "Yes, that's us. Can we help you?"

"I'm here to help you, Mr. Pollard and Mr. Barsotti. I'm Vanesa Galloway, second chair on this case. I've been very involved since the beginning and asked Mr. Touré if I could handle the interview today so that I could meet both of you personally." After shaking both of our hands, she added, "We should probably head back. Mr. Mazer is waiting on us."

We went through the same routine, placing all our things at the front desk except for our notepad and pen. As Vanesa led us back through the concrete maze, Lewis gave me a nudge and a pointed look. Now I knew that he noticed my jaw on the floor. He gave me a thumbs-up and that big grin of his. I replied by tapping the notebook to let him know I was only interested in the work. But she had caught me off guard, at least for a moment, and triggered a strange sense of déjà vu.

When we entered the room, Craig looked as malnourished and sleep deprived as before, but there was a calmness to him today. Vanesa walked around the table and gave Craig a hug, which it seemed like he needed. I took a mental note that she believed in her client because I doubt she would be hugging someone she believed to be a murderer. Lewis and I each shook Craig's hand and then took our seats across the table from him.

Craig spoke up first. "I know I lost my composure last time, but I'll get through all your questions today. I've been through a lot, but I'm dealing with it better each day, little by little. What more do you need to know from me?"

"Today, Mr. Mazer, we're going to ask you about Dogon Tech, your alibi, and Grant Dogon. Let's start with your alibi. You said that you were working, but we know that the security system was down. What were you working on so late? Was there anyone else there who saw you there?"

"I was there working on the numbers for the public offering. We must produce all our business financials for the initial price of the stock. I had some numbers that weren't matching up over the last couple of months, and I have—well, had—to figure out what was going on and where the discrepancies were. I've been working late most nights because of the added responsibilities of a higher role in the company, like I told you before. It's what caused some of the problems with my wife."

He got quiet and almost whispered his next sentence, "No, I didn't see anyone that night."

"Craig, what were the discrepancies? Is Grant hiding something?" Lewis chimed in for the first time.

Before he answered, Craig glanced at Vanesa. She nodded her head to answer. "Well, there seems to have been some inflated numbers on the reports, and they weren't matching with the output. When I approached Grant about them, he gave me explanations on each one, but it still never seemed to match completely. In the end, I did my job and made the corrections in the reports and made them match with the higher numbers."

"How many times have you had to 'fix' the numbers, as you put it? How did you do this?"

"Over the last three months, I have *corrected* the numbers seven times, including the night my wife was murdered while I was *working*! I worked until 2:30 A.M. and got home around 3 A.M. I go through all of our output and compare the numbers to the sale price on the income. There was not enough output for the sales numbers, but Grant told me that the buyers had added more products after the initial reported numbers. At least, that was the story that night."

"OK, Craig, I hear you. Let's move on to what's happening with the security system. Why is it shutting down? We know that it happened more often than the night of your wife's murder."

"I'm not really sure. I'm not a tech guy; I only work at a tech company. The IT department has assured me that it's just a glitch in the system from when they updated the software. They told me it would be fixed before the public offering. That's all I can tell you about it."

I turned to Lewis and whispered, "Is that the same story you got from Jack Gaither?"

He quickly nodded his head, and I continued with the interview. "Mr. Mazer, with all the technology out there today, what about geo location on your phone or car?"

"Unfortunately, they are all company owned and under the same security system as the building. If it's down, so is our tracking systems on our company technology."

"OK, I understand, Mr. Mazer." I felt like Craig knew more, but I didn't think we would get any more out of him. And I really wanted to hear what he had to say about Grant. "Can you tell us about you and Grant, your relationship after the military and his relationship with your wife?"

"Grant has always been there for me. He led and protected our platoon while serving, and he gave me everything I have when we got back. He gave me a life, a job, and helped me meet Helen. Every time that I have struggled with my new position, he's helped me make the transition with all my duties as an executive. He's also the one who got me through each of the discrepancies, every time, talking me through the numbers and explaining how it worked. I can't say a bad word about the man."

"I understand your respect for Grant, but you said something about him helping you meet Helen?" We knew the story but wanted to see if it matched up.

"Yes, I didn't know at the time, but later as things progressed with Helen, Grant told me he arranged our meeting. I didn't believe him at first, but after he explained how he was able to make sure that we were working together at the event where we met, I decided it was too big of a coincidence otherwise. Also, he's known Helen since high school."

"Thank you for your time, Mr. Mazer. I hope that as we get deeper into this, you'll allow us to come back and speak to you again."

Again, we all shook hands, and Vanesa led us back to the front. She said that she was heading back in to go over the case with her client and hoped that she would see us again soon. I hoped so too.

CHAPTER 16

AS LEWIS AND I got back into the car, he had that silly grin again. But before he said anything, I snapped at his driver, "Take us to Dogon Tech, please."

"Angelo, what's the plan? I'm with you, but how do you want to do this? Who are we going to see there?"

"I want you to introduce me to Jack Gaither, and then I want you to follow my lead."

"Got it, Boss."

■ ■ ■

After the car pulled up to Dogon Tech, we strode in through the massive glass doors. The entire building was made of metallic-tinted glass. It gave off that "we are a tech company" vibe. We approached the front desk, which could have sat about eight people with its size, but there was just one woman. A security guard was posted at each side of the desk, with scanning systems just past them. Everyone in or out had to scan a key card at the system.

Lewis asked for Jack Gaither. The woman at the front desk asked if we had an appointment. I replied, "No, but if you would tell him that Angelo Barsotti and Lewis Pollard were here, I'm sure he would gladly see us." She begrudgingly called up, and after a few seconds, she handed Lewis and I visitor passes and told us he would meet us at the elevator on the twenty-second floor. As we headed to the elevator, the security guard on our side of the desk said that we needed to scan in with our visitor badges.

We rode up the copper-finished elevator straight up to the twenty-second floor where Jack Gaither was waiting. He was built like Grant, a little shorter, but not much. But he also had a weathered face, like he used to be a smoker or something. And his hair was nothing like Grant's; it had an intentionally messy look in a sandy light brown. Lewis shook hands with him first and then introduced me.

"How can we help you today, gentlemen?" he asked in a gruff but friendly tone.

This time I spoke, "Jack, we would like for you to take us to the IT department. We'd like to get a better handle on the shutdowns that are occurring, or glitches, as they're being called."

"Well, I've been personally overseeing that, so I can help you. What is it that you'd like to know?"

"First off, we'd like to know how many shutdowns there have been and, if you could, give us the dates of each shutdown. Also, why are they occurring? Is there any explanation?"

"We've identified the reason behind the glitches. That *is* what they are—a glitch in the system causing all security to shut down. We lose cameras, computers, and all our locks through-out the building, and geo location services on all employee technology products, like cars and cell phones. We've had to hire extra on-call security to man the building when these glitches happen to ensure we have no intruders. There have been eight such glitches in the last three months, including last night. They're being caused by a software update, which we're working on fixing as we speak. As for the dates, I'll have to get that information over to you once I get it from the IT department and I get clearance from Mr. Dogon."

Lewis took his chance to chime in, "As you told me before, Grant said to help us as much as possible. I think you can get the dates for us now."

"You're right, Lewis, Mr. Dogon did tell me to help, but he also instructed me to clear anything about the security glitches with him first. Until we can figure out what's going on, all things must go through him. Look, gentlemen, can I help you with anything else? I'm a very busy person and must get back to my duties unless you need anything else from me."

"Thank you for your time, Mr. Gaither. We look forward to getting those dates from you as soon as possible. Lewis and I can show ourselves out."

CHAPTER 17

AS SOON AS WE were in the car, Lewis asked me, "Why did you let him off so easy? I think we could have gotten more from him."

"Lewis, I let him off for now. I want you to find out everything you can about Jack Gaither. Jack and Grant are hiding something. They both appear to want to be helpful, but only with what they want us to know. They won't let us get close to Dogon Tech and what's happening there. And there is definitely something happening there. Now I need you to drop me off at the bar for my shift tonight. I'm going to try and find out more on who else the police were looking at before they settled on Craig and stopped looking at the other two people of interest or anyone else they had suspicions of."

■ ■ ■

When my alarm went off the next morning, I shot Lewis a text that I was up. He had left me a voice mail that he'd found something out about Jack. He immediately texted back that he was on his way over. It must be something big because it was way too early for Lewis to be up and about already.

I put on a pot of coffee and waited for Lewis to show up. I hadn't gotten anything out of the police last night. They told me to stop trying to poke holes in their case; Craig was their guy. They said that the other two people of interest were no longer of interest because their alibies were solid, but they wouldn't give me any hints as to who they were. They started getting upset that I was trying to undo their police work, and I decided to back off for the night.

Lewis walked in without knocking and started right in, "Jack Gaither was part of the platoon that Craig and Grant were on, except then his name was James Grayson. Apparently, James Grayson was dishonorably discharged for trying to steal government technology. They didn't have enough to prove it, so he was never charged with anything, but he was kicked out. To get out from under the cloud of suspicion, he changed his name and reached out to Grant for a job. Also, there was a rumor that he was covering for his direct lead when trying to steal the technology, but that was also never proven. Do you know who his direct lead was?"

"Grant Dogon."

"Right, Grant Dogon. It would seem Mr. Gaither is in the business of covering for his boss whenever necessary. And Grant Dogon pays him very well for it. He has made almost as much as Grant in every company that he has worked with him— even more than Craig, who's supposed to be his number two."

"Lewis, this is good, but it doesn't mean anything for sure. We need to go back to Craig and talk to him about Jack/James."

"Already on it, Boss. We have a meeting with Miss Vanesa for dinner tonight to discuss what we've found out and to set up another meeting with Mr. Mazer." He paused, adding mischievously, "And maybe make a little connection for you and her…"

"Lewis, don't start with that; we're on a case. A murder case. We need to make sure the right person is found, if in fact it's not Mr. Mazer. And if it's not Craig, we need to get him out immediately."

"Fine, fine, business as usual. But don't close your heart off forever." As he was walking out, he said, "Oh yeah, Angelo, dress up. We're going to Mastro's Steakhouse."

CHAPTER 18

LEWIS SENT A CAR for me, but he wasn't in it. He sent me a text that he would meet us there. I came up to the restaurant hostess and asked for the reservation for Mr. Pollard. The hostess said, "Yes, right this way, Mr. Pollard. Your guest is already here."

I didn't bother correcting her and instead followed her to the table. She led me all the way to the back, and as we approached the table, I noticed Vanesa was already seated. She looked unbelievable. She didn't look like a lawyer at all—more like a cover girl. Her dress hugged her in all the right places, and those eyes captured me again. Tonight, she had a little more subtle nose ring, but it was perfect. Then I noticed something else—the table was only set for two.

I awkwardly said hello to Vanesa, and even more awkwardly accepted a hug from her. She said that Lewis texted that he would not be making it, but she thought I knew that already. She must have noticed the confusion on my face.

The waiter came to the table and greeted us, "Hello, Miss Galloway, Mr. Barsotti. Mr. Pollard is very sorry he cannot join you tonight, but he said that the bill is on him. He insisted on you starting with a bottle of wine from our reserved list."

He handed us a wine list that was not on the table. It had a hard leather-covered book with an embossed logo of the restaurant. "So, what would you like?"

I looked at Vanesa and said, "Lady's choice."

She perused the list and decided on an amazing cabernet from Napa Valley. This was off to a good start. It's like she knew exactly what I would've ordered.

We exchanged small talk as we waited for the wine to come. Hopefully that would loosen me up some. I'm horrible at small talk, especially with new people, and especially when I have butterflies every time I meet her eyes. When the waiter arrived with our wine, he was followed by a man carrying crab cakes and a wagyu beef roll from the sushi selection. "Mr. Pollard has already ordered a set menu for you both, and I promise, it will not disappoint. Main courses will come out in a bit, but here are some of our most popular appetizers to start. Please enjoy."

As soon as the waiter was out of earshot, I said, "Leave it to Lewis to take control even without being here."

Vanesa laughed and said, "It's nice. Now we can just talk and not worry about what we're going to order."

"I guess you're right. We do have some new information and would really like to speak to Mr. Mazer again."

I told her all about Jack/James and the shutdowns. I also hinted to her that there appeared to be as many shutdowns as there were discrepancies but were waiting on the dates from both Craig and Jack to compare. She listened to every word without saying a thing, almost as if she already knew all this. But I continued anyways, as it helped me make my own connections when I could talk through things.

Once I had finished and we had finished the appetizers, she finally said, "Look, Angelo, there are things in this case that we cannot let out. They're major points for our defense of Mr. Mazer. I'm completely behind him, and I don't believe he killed his wife. So, I apologize if you feel that we have misled you and Lewis in any way, but we must do what's best for our client."

The chef brought out our main course: two 18-ounce bone-in filets with lobster mashed potatoes and brussels sprouts. We ate in silence for a bit, mainly because the food was excellent, but also because I didn't want to get upset with her that they withheld information from us—information that could help us get to the bottom of what happened.

When we finished the steaks and sides that Lewis had ordered, Vanesa spoke first, "Angelo, I have another confession. I asked Lewis if it could be just the two of us tonight."

I sat there dumbstruck, so she quickly spoke again, "I really wanted to get to know you. More than I already do. I've been following your wife's murder case since it happened. And once I met you, I was infatuated. I admit, I have a little crush on you. So, when Lewis called and said he wanted to get together and go over the case, I asked him if he minded if it was the two of us. Lewis thought it was a great idea, but I feel a little embarrassed about it."

"Well, since we're confessing, I was completely caught off guard by you; you're beautiful and smart. However, and I don't mean this as a rejection, but I must focus on the case right now."

She peered at me with those dazzling blue eyes and simply replied, "I completely agree."

We ordered another bottle of wine and talked about our lives. She graduated from Columbia Law School and immediately started working for Mr. Touré, eventually becoming a top lawyer there. She hoped to become a partner soon. She had been engaged twice previously, but neither worked out. I told her about life as a PI, my marriage, and my bartending at a cop bar for information. I told her how Lewis and I met and the silly boyhood story of Roy McGinty. We talked easily for a couple hours, then I walked her out to her chauffeur. Apparently, Lewis had sent a car for her too.

She gave me a hug and a kiss on the cheek and said, "Call me when this is over, and maybe we can have a proper date." She slipped a note into my coat pocket with her phone number and lightly caressed my hand.

She left me standing there speechless and emotionally a wreck. I owed it to myself to move on, but obviously, I hadn't found closure yet. I waited for my car, deep in thought, and then went home and fell fast asleep but not before I sent a text to Lewis that simply said, "Thanks."

CHAPTER 19

THE NEXT MORNING, I got up feeling a little hungover and very confused with how I felt or should be feeling. I stumbled over to my jacket and pulled out the slip of paper that Vanesa had slipped into my pocket at the end of the night. I put her number in my phone but also included "Mr. Mazer's lawyer" in the contact. When I set the piece of paper down, I had somehow flipped it over. On the back was a note that said:

I have some thoughts and some clues about your wife's murder that no one else knows. PLEASE help me get through this case, and I will help you completely.
~Vanesa

Whoa! I thought I was confused before, but now…what the hell? OK, I've waited over two years to get some answers about what happened that night, so I guess I could wait a little longer. My initial reaction was to pick up the phone and call Vanesa immediately to grill her, but I didn't think she would even answer. I needed to call Lewis. I needed to think. What a cluster!

I decided to sit for a while and let it all sink in and the wine fog to clear before I did anything. My head was spinning, and I couldn't figure out if it was from the wine, my mixed emotions, or the cryptic note about my wife. I tried to sort through my thoughts.

I decided to make a pros and cons list about pushing Vanesa to share what she knew about my wife's murder.

PROS	CONS
I could possibly find my wife's murderer.	Mr. Mazer goes to jail for a crime he may not have committed.
I could get closure.	I don't do all I can do for a client.
	I lose my reputation.
	I don't respect Vanesa's wishes to see this case through.

The cons outweighed the pros, and all the pros were completely selfish. If I pursued my wife's murder right now, it would only be for me, and I would be letting everyone else down. I needed to finish the case because I said I would, so that's what I intended to do. But, man, this was going to be hard to not think about.

I called Lewis, but I decided not to tell him about Vanesa's note. He would only want to pursue it, and I wanted to see this case through first. I *must* see this through first. I can't put someone else's life ahead of my own satisfaction.

Lewis playfully teased me about my date and how he set it all up, and I let him have his fun. Then I told him that we would meet with Craig today at 2:30 P.M. He replied that he would have a car at my apartment at one, and he would be in it this time.

CHAPTER 20

WE ONCE AGAIN WERE at the jail. I was feeling very anxious to see Vanesa because I didn't know what to say or how to act. But the case comes first. And I hadn't told Lewis about the note, so I wouldn't say anything in front of him anyways.

When Mr. Touré walked out from the back, Lewis and I gave each other a puzzled look. I said, "I thought we were meeting Vanesa—I mean, Miss Galloway."

"I was under that impression too." Mr. Touré replied. "She set this meeting up. She hasn't even caught me up with what you all talked about last night. Actually, no one has seen her since last night. She left a short voice mail on the company line that said she needed some time off and that was it. It's not like her to do this in the middle of an important case. Did something happen last night that I need to know about?"

"Not that I know of," I said. "We had a nice evening and talked about the case. Basically, I told her what we had found out about Jack Gaither, or rather, James Grayson, but it seems that you both already knew about that connection. Then she got in her car that Lewis had sent for her and that was it."

"Well, it does worry me some, but we must move on today without her, I'm afraid. I'll call into the office as soon as we're done and see if they have heard anything else from her. Let's head back to Mr. Mazer, please."

"Just one minute." I frantically tried calling Vanesa's phone but got the operator message that the phone was no longer in service. "Shit!"

"What?" both Lewis and Mr. Touré said in unison.

"Her phone is turned off or out of service. I'm sure she's OK. She did call into the office and said she needed time off, so I guess we need to go with that for now."

We went through the same routine with security and the same pleasantries with Craig. Then I jumped right in, "Mr. Mazer, we're not here to take a lot of your time, but we do need some answers to a pressing matter within Dogon Tech. Who is James Grayson to you?"

Again, like before, he had a deer-in-the-headlights moment but quickly recovered. "Do you mean Jack Gaither? He doesn't go by James Grayson anymore. He was in our platoon, and Grant has kept all of us close since we got out. Jack has been with us since Grant and I got back from deployment. And since you know his real name, I'm sure you already know that James was kicked out for allegedly trying to steal government technology. But they didn't have enough evidence to prove it, so he was quietly let go with a dishonorable discharge. He didn't like having a smudge in his record and neither did Grant. So, they fixed the problem so that we could all work together again. What does he have to do with this? I've already told this to my lawyers."

"Well, Mr. Mazer, you didn't tell us," Lewis said pointedly. "Jack oversees the security issues. He said that there were eight shutdowns in the last three months, including one the other night, and there were seven nights you remember finding discrepancies. So, there have been seven shutdowns before your arrest and one after. Did you remember the dates of those discrepancies that we asked you for?"

I added, "What Lewis is trying to put nicely is that we need those dates urgently. Jack is gathering the dates of the shutdowns now, and we want to know if they match the nights that you found discrepancies and reported them to Mr. Dogon. We have a feeling that the shutdowns are not glitches, like they're being presented, but are being done intentionally."

Craig looked shocked as he asked, "Why would they do that?"

"Because, Mr. Mazer, we think they are covering up things they don't want known or could get out to the public. We think that it has to do with the public offering. But right now, all we have are our suspicions, but we'd like to get evidence."

"But how does that help clear me of my wife's murder?"

"Unfortunately, we're not sure that it does, but for now, we're following this where it leads us."

CHAPTER 21

WHEN WE STEPPED OUT of the jail, my phone pinged. It was a text from an unknown sender, which read:

> I know you're in meeting with Craig, and I wanted to let you know that I'm ok for now. I'll call you soon with more, but that's all I can tell you right now. –V

I felt relief and worry all at once. Why would she need to let me know she was OK? Was she running from something that could put her in danger? I hoped she would call soon.

Lewis snapped me out of my thoughts. "Are you OK?"

"Yeah, I'm just trying to piece all this together. We need to talk to Grant again."

"Back to Dogon Tech?"

"No, we need to have him on neutral turf. I don't think he'll give us much in front of his employees or the cameras in his offices."

■ ■ ■

We met Grant in Central Park. He said that he didn't have long, as he had a company to run, but for Craig, he would meet us. I had a plan and asked Lewis to pay close attention to Grant as I talked.

"Grant, we just met with Craig again. And we met with Mr. Gaither yesterday. Or should I say, James Grayson?"

Grant looked dumbfounded, but I didn't let him speak—not yet.

"Why is Jack in charge of the security issues? Is he covering for you again? Because we know that each time there was a so-called glitch, it matches the date that Mr. Mazer approached you with inflated numbers. Can you tell us why this is?"

Grant stammered, "How could you know the dates matched up? I told Jack not to give you that information!" His anger was rising but knew that there were too many people around to begin yelling. He took a deep breath and continued, "Look, Mr. Barsotti, I'm not sure what you're getting at, but that simply isn't true. Our IT department has assured us that there is a glitch that they are fixing as we speak! Did you come here to ambush me with accusations about my company? I'm paying you to get the murder charge off Craig, not to investigate how I run my business. I'm finished with this conversation! Please get back to what I hired you for."

As Grant stormed off, I whispered, "Oh, I think we're just getting started."

CHAPTER 22

BACK IN THE CAR, Lewis laughed and thanked me for the show. He asked me why I put it out there that we knew the dates matched when we didn't have a clue. I told him that we needed answers, and we got it, even though the people we were asking didn't want to give us the answers. So, we got the dates without ever actually getting the dates. We both saw it in Grant's face and how he responded that we were right.

My phone pinged, unknown sender:

> I will call you soon. Please answer! –V

"Lewis, can you take me home? I'm going to call it an early night. I think we got a lot of information today, but the real work is still ahead of us."

"Of course. Nice work today, Angelo. You surprise me on every case with some of the tricks you pull. You know how to pull the right strings at the right time to get people to give you what we need."

"Thanks, Lewis."

Right when I walked into my apartment, my phone started ringing from a blocked number. I answered it before it could ring a second time.

"Where are you?" I asked a little more crazily than I'd wanted.

"I'm not sure who you were expecting, Angelo, but this is Grant. I want you to get Craig out of jail. I hired you because you're a small-time investigator and should know better than to stick your nose where it doesn't belong. Stop digging before someone else gets hurt!"

He hung up before I could say anything. Well, at least I now knew why he hired me. But he didn't know me. I wouldn't stop until I got to the bottom of this, regardless of his threats.

I fell asleep holding my phone, waiting for the call that didn't come. My phone text message ping woke me up though:

I'm sorry! I will call eventually, but I can't yet. Sorry. –V

CHAPTER 23

MY NIGHT HADN'T GONE as I expected, but I now knew for sure that we were on the right track. Grant's phone call confirmed that something bad was going on in that company, and he wanted to make a huge profit off the public offering before anyone found out. He was willing to tell lies and conceal information to protect himself and his company. What else was he willing to do?

As for Vanesa, as long as she continued to text, at least I knew that she was OK. She was conflicted about something, and I thought it had to do with my wife's murder. I wanted to talk to her, but she would reach out when she was ready, I guess. Besides, I had another murder to solve first.

I called Lewis and filled him in on the fun phone call I received the night before. He asked, "How are we going to handle Grant Dogon? I got your back, Boss, but we need a plan."

"No more busting down doors, but we're definitely not stopping or backing down. I think whatever is going on at Dogon Tech has something to do with Helen Mazer's murder. Why don't you come over? I have another plan. Oh, and bring $2,000 of Grant's money with you."

An Army of Lies ▪ 71

▪ ▪ ▪

Lewis was over within an hour. He had a duffle bag with Grant's money in it. While I was waiting on Lewis, I had called Mr. Touré and told him to ask Craig a question, and he had already gotten back to me.

"I hope your driver is still here. We're going to lunch."

"With whom?"

"I'll explain on the way. Bring the bag."

▪ ▪ ▪

On the way to Katz's Delicatessen, I called Cal Dunst, the head of the IT department at Dogon Tech, and asked if he would meet us for lunch. I knew Katz's was a five-minute walk from Dogon, and it's a busy place, perfect for a conversation that would get lost in the noise. He said sure because he was told to help in any way possible. Grant must not have paid him a visit yet, which worked in our favor. Grant was probably typing up a memo as we rode to lunch to not talk to us about anything that has to do with Dogon Tech unless approved by him.

I filled Lewis in on my plan and who we were meeting. Traffic, as usual, was very congested, so we decided to walk the last few blocks so Mr. Dunst wouldn't think we were a no-show.

When we were getting close to the restaurant, we saw a skinny young kid, maybe twenty-five, waving at us. He had wavy blond hair and was dressed like a hipster. I thought, how could this be the head of the IT department for a major technology company?

I asked, "Are you Cal Dunst?"

"Yes. Nice to meet you, Mr. Barsotti and Mr. Pollard."

"You can call us Angelo and Lewis. By the way, how old are you? You look to be too young to be running the IT department at Dogon Tech!"

"I get that all the time, but long story short, I was a computer whiz and graduated college when I was sixteen with a degree in computer science. I also have a master's in multiple computer technologies, and I was recruited by Dogon to run their IT department. All that to say I'm twenty-three, and yes, I oversee the IT department."

"Impressive. Can we buy you lunch?"

"Sure."

We all got in line and each ordered the pastrami sandwich, which is freshly sliced in nice big chunks of meat. The corned beef is a close second, but pastrami is the way to go. Once our food was ready, we found a table in the back that a group had just vacated.

"Cal, we wanted to talk to you about the security issues that are causing shutdowns. What's going on?"

After finishing a mouthful, Cal started reciting the script we had heard before: "There's a glitch in the new software update that I installed about three months ago. I've just finished uninstalling it and rebooting the software to get a newer version, and all should be smooth sailing now."

"Look, Cal, we've heard the exact same story from multiple people, and it doesn't work for us. You're telling me that a major technology firm with a genius running its IT department would let this go on for three months when all you needed to do was to uninstall the software update, an update that was causing shutdowns of all security measures and leaving the company completely vulnerable? No way; it doesn't add up."

Cal looked squeamish, like someone had punched him in the stomach. He stopped eating and studied his food like it was going to give him the answer. I discreetly nodded to Lewis, so he chimed in, "Hey, I know it's not a lot, but if you could tell us what's really going on, I have $1,000 cash in this bag that could be yours."

Cal glanced around the restaurant and finally said, "You're right, but we can't talk here. Let's take a walk."

They wrapped up their food, threw it into to-go bags, and proceeded outside. They walked in the opposite direction of Dogon Tech. After about two blocks, Cal started talking.

"Look, guys, I don't need the money, I just need to get this off my chest. I've been holding on to all of this for three months, and I can't do it anymore. Once Craig was charged with murder, on a night of a glitch, I knew I had to tell someone. So, here it goes. There is no glitch. It's a manual shutdown of all security, and the only person who has the power to do that is Mr. Dogon. I went to him the first time it happened. I thought maybe he accidentally did it somehow, but I found out otherwise. I don't know why he's doing it, but he told me that I was to tell no one and to figure out a way to explain it all away. So, I came up with the idea of the glitch. If anyone had spent some time on it, they would have figured it out, but everyone relies on me to figure it out for them. The glitch was born, and I was to report all glitches to Jack Gaither. I wish I knew more of the why, but I hope that helps."

"Cal, that helps a lot. Maybe when we wrap this up, we can buy you lunch again and tell you the whys. But for now, go on acting like you told no one, but you may want to start looking for a new job. I'm not sure Dogon Tech will survive this when it's all over."

"Don't worry about me, Mr. Barsotti. You know, genius and all that. I have options."

They watched Cal walk back the way they came, headed back to Dogon. I hoped he could keep it quiet that he told us. I really didn't want anything to happen to him.

CHAPTER 24

LEWIS AND I STRATEGIZED what to do next on the car ride back to my apartment. We decided that we needed to go back to visit Craig but let him know this was the last time, so we needed the absolute truth. We wanted to make him feel backed into a corner. If he didn't tell us the truth, then we would be done with his case. Lewis said he would set it up with Mr. Touré.

When we pulled up to my apartment, Lewis said he had another one of his events to get ready for. I asked him what this one was for. He answered, "It's an overpriced dinner to raise money for the elephants in Africa. If we just donated the money that we spent on the dinner, we would help a lot more elephants. But hey, it's an open bar, and I'll know people there."

"Will Grant Dogon be there?"

"No, that isn't his scene. Why?"

"Could I tag along tonight? I really need to clear my head and be away from anything familiar."

"Of course, Boss. I'll pick you up at six. Wear your tux."

I shuffled up the sidewalk to my apartment entrance, dreading the night ahead, but I needed a night away from my life, away from the case. No Mr. Mazer. No Vanesa. No wondering about my wife's murder. Just Lewis and a bunch of people I didn't know. And an open bar. I'm not a big drinker, but free drinks are the best.

I only had a couple of hours to get ready, so I took a few minutes to jot down notes of Cal's version of events. Then I decided to take a quick nap because a night out with Lewis could turn into morning real fast.

When I woke up, I had just enough time to put myself together before Lewis would arrive. I pulled out my tuxedo, a gray pocket square (for the elephants, of course), black socks, and my shiny black shoes. I don't dress up often; I like to be comfortable in what I wear. But when I put on my ensemble and fixed my hair, I didn't look half bad. I liked the fact that my hair hadn't started graying yet, and I tried to keep in shape as much as possible. I checked the mirror one more time as I waited for Lewis.

Lewis texted me that he was here, and for once, I decided to leave my phone at home. I knew there was a chance Vanesa could call, but I really needed the night off from everything. I hoped she would understand once I do talk to her—if she even called.

■ ■ ■

For the first couple of hours, I stood near wherever Lewis was holding court. He always had a crowd around him, and I could get lost in the background. But as the drinks continued to flow, I gained some confidence. I still placed myself within Lewis's group, but I was a full participant in the conversations. Sometimes I probably spoke up a little too much. Lewis could tell I was letting go and having fun, so he let me just keep going.

As the night was winding down, I figured out that I had had a lot to drink. My big clue was that I was dancing. There wasn't even a dance floor, but there was music. And when I drink and the music is on, I like to dance. I'm not the greatest dancer, but people always join in with me because they can tell I'm having a great time. They want to have a great time too, so we all let loose and have a dance party to cap off the night.

Lewis pulled me out of there before I became too much of a fool. I slept most of the way home. Lewis woke me up to tell me that we were at my apartment, and he asked if I could make it up to my bed by myself. I told him that I could and said, "Thanks, Lewis. I needed this. Tomorrow, we get right back to it. Love you, brother. Good night."

CHAPTER 25

MORNING CAME HARD AND fast. My world was spinning a little, and I had a bad headache. The sun seemed like a spotlight shining directly in my eyes. And when I picked up my phone, I realized that Vanesa had called and texted quite a bit over the previous night. Unfortunately, I had no way to get back in touch with her because even my replies to her texts were being blocked. I felt bad, mainly because maybe she needed me and I wasn't there for her.

While I was holding my phone, it pinged. It was Lewis, saying to be ready in an hour. He had set up the meeting with Craig, but Lewis decided we needed to get some food in us first.

When I got in the car, Lewis said we were going to Hahm Ji Bach to get their Gamjatang. It's known as the hangover soup, and I couldn't wait. It's a little bit of a drive but worth it. I wasn't sure if it was really a hangover cure, but I always felt better after eating it.

My phone started ringing—unknown number. I said, "Hello?" It was Vanesa. She replied, "Angelo! I've been calling since last night!"

"I know, I'm so sorry. I unplugged last night and left my phone at home. I really needed a break from everything. Again, I'm truly sorry."

"It's OK, Angelo. I understand. I wish I could take a break from life too sometimes."

"Where are you, and what's going on, Vanesa?"

"I can't tell you an answer to either of those yet, but I did want to tell you that I found out that Grant Dogon is manually shutting down the system. There are no glitches."

"We just found that out as well. How did you find out?"

"I called over to Dogon Tech and spoke to a man named Cal Dunst, head of the IT department. He told me that he had already told someone about it, but I wasn't sure it was you. He wouldn't tell me who he told, but he knew I was Craig's lawyer and wanted to help. I know you're meeting with Craig today, so I wanted to make sure you had that information. I guess I was a little behind with this one. Sorry I can't be there to help out."

"Why can't you, though? What is happening?"

"For now, Angelo, all I can say safely is that the people who murdered your wife are after me now. There's so much more I wish I could tell you, but it's not safe right now."

"Wait! What? My wife was murdered intentionally? She was the target? Not a burglary gone wrong. Vanesa, how can you know this?"

But she wasn't there. She must have hung up as I asked my questions. I sat there in a total state of shock. *What is going on?* At that same moment, Lewis asked the same thing, "Angelo! What is going on?"

I decided it was time to tell him about the Vanesa situation. "OK, Lewis, I should have probably told you right away, but I was focused on this case, and I wanted it to stay that way. When I had dinner with Vanesa, she slipped me a note when she left that said she knew things about Lucy's murder. That she had clues to who it was that no one else knows. And then she skipped town. And now she just told me that she's on the run from the same people who murdered Lucy. It wasn't some random act; she was murdered for a reason," I concluded, feeling in a daze.

"Angelo, I'm sorry. I can't understand how we're just now finding out about this. I do wish you had told me right away. Maybe I could have helped Vanesa; I could have helped you. But I understand why you didn't. Sometimes, Angelo, you have a one-track mind, and sometimes that's good, but other times, it makes you miss what's right in front of you. You have people who can help you, and I'm one of them. Next time, depend on me."

"I got it, Lewis. Again, I'm sorry. I knew that you would want to move on this information that Vanesa could possibly give us about Lucy, but I must finish this for Craig, and for Helen. Then we can deal with my wife's murder."

"OK, Boss, but with your permission, I'm going to put some resources into finding Vanesa and at least protect her until this case is wrapped up."

"Agreed."

■ ■ ■

The soup was amazing, as always, and it helped to clear my head, at least of the alcohol and toxins. As for the cluster of things running through my mind, those still needed to be sorted out. That would start with Craig.

I told Lewis the way to handle Craig this time. "No more kid gloves, no more coddling. We need to back him into a corner, one he cannot escape from. He needs to stop protecting others and look out for himself."

"You're right, Angelo. We've been treating him like the victim, which he is, but not treating him like someone we are trying to get out of jail. He may get upset, he may push back, but we need to break him for his own good."

CHAPTER 26

MR. TOURÉ WAS READY and waiting for us. We called him ahead of time to prep Craig for what was to come. We wanted Craig to be ready and willing to answer the questions we had for him. We also wanted him to know this was his last chance to be honest about everything.

This time when we entered the room, there were no handshakes or pleasantries. Craig looked totally stressed and fatigued. I started right in on him, "Mr. Mazer, you should know by now why we're here again. I hope that you took Mr. Touré's advice and are ready to talk because if you hold anything back any more than you already have, we will be done here. Do you understand?"

He nodded slowly in response. I said, "Mr. Mazer, we're going back to the night of the murder. Where were you when your wife was killed?"

"Like I said before, I was at work. Do we have to go over the same questions?"

"Yes, until we get the truth. Before you said no one else was there, but you also said you had a discrepancy that night and that you talked to Mr. Dogon about each time that you had a discrepancy. So, was Mr. Dogon at Dogon Tech the night your wife was killed? Think hard before you lie to us."

Craig's eyes shifted around the room but couldn't meet any of our eyes. Eventually, he looked right at me, defeated. "Yes, he was there. He was also there when I left."

"Why did you lie to us before?"

"When I came to him after the police questioned me, he told me that I could not tell anyone that he was at work. He said that it could ruin the business and the public offering. I still don't understand why it would ruin the business, but I'm loyal to a fault. Grant was always there for me, so I had to be there for him, whatever he asked."

"He could have been your alibi! This all would have been put to rest about you being the murderer. And what's worse is that you don't even know the real reason Mr. Dogon didn't want you telling anyone that he was there. Every time you presented him with a discrepancy, he erased the security system so that no one saw you two talking over inflated numbers. He wasn't worried about you. He was worried that someone would find what you found and wanted all records of it gone. There were no glitches; it was all Mr. Dogon protecting his company. Instead of protecting you, he's only looking out for himself!"

"No! He wouldn't do that! He told me that the discrepancies were just errors. That the files were wrong and needed to be fixed. And that the security system was all a software problem. I even personally confirmed all of this with Cal Dunst!"

"Well, Mr. Mazer, we've talked to Mr. Dunst as well. He's recanted his version of events and told us the truth; Grant Dogon was manually resetting the system and getting rid of whatever went on those nights in the office. He said Mr. Dogon was the only one who could do this and that he was told to make up a plausible story to feed everyone who asked about it. So, like you, Cal was a follower. Until he decided that things needed to be fixed. He even went as far to say that you were the reason he needed to tell someone because the system was erased the night of your wife's murder. He confirmed it could have protected you, showing that you were in fact where you said you were. So, Craig, again I'm asking you, was anyone else there that night?"

"Yes, Jack Gaither."

"Wait, Jack could have been another alibi? You would have never even gone to jail!"

"No, no. He didn't see me. He arrived very late, around 2 A.M.; I saw him hurriedly walk by my office to Grant's office. He didn't notice me there. And when I went to leave, they were in a very animated conversation, so I didn't even say bye."

Craig began rocking back and forth, becoming visibly angry and agitated. He started whispering, more to himself than to us, "That liar. After all I've done for him, he's been lying to me. Liar. Liar. LIAR!" The last one was almost a full yell.

"Craig, calm down. We're on your side, but we need to figure out who killed your wife to get you out of this now. Because even if we got Mr. Dogon to come forward as your alibi now, they wouldn't believe him. We're thinking that your wife's murder has something to do with Dogon Tech and its public offering. Can you think of any reason she would be connected to the company?"

"NO! She isn't involved in the company, and I don't—sorry, didn't—even talk to her about the company. She said she didn't want to hear about the place that took me away from her."

"OK, well, thank you for finally being completely transparent with us, and we're sorry for you having to find out these things from us. If you think of anything else that you haven't shared with us already, please get ahold of Mr. Touré immediately. And hopefully the next time we talk, it will be because we're getting you out of here."

CHAPTER 27

LEWIS STARTED TALKING AS soon as we were in the car. "Nice work in there! You got him to tell us all that he was holding back. Also, while you were at work in there, my guys have located Vanesa. They have a perimeter set up, and she'll have no clue that they are there. She's in a time-share cabin that is registered to her parents in Vermont. They have booked a full month, but they're at home in New York. She's smart having them book it for her and not in her own name. We must be careful, though, because if we found her, someone else can too"

"Great! And thank you, Lewis."

"Not a problem. So, how are we going to figure out who murdered Helen Mazer?"

"Right now, we need to keep following this Dogon Tech trail, and I think it will take us to our conclusion, or at least part of it."

■ ■ ■

Lewis dropped me off at my place. He was going to meet with his guys that were running the operation to protect Vanesa and strategize for an extract as soon as this case was closed. I was going to work on how to get Grant to talk. He wasn't going to let us barge into Dogon Tech and let us look around anymore.

My phone started ringing from an unknown number. "Hello?"

"Angelo, I'm still safe. And I have another bit of information that I was able to get out of my friends in the police department. There were two other people of interest besides Craig Mazer when they began their investigation."

"Yes, we knew that too. But we couldn't get their names."

"Right, well I did! My contact in the department let me know the names: Grant Dogon and Jack Gaither!"

"Well, that is interesting! How were they dismissed as suspects? Were you able to get that information as well?"

"Of course, Angelo. I don't do things halfway. Their alibis checked out. They were apparently at a bar, Attaboy, until 3 A.M. They each had receipts to prove it. Seems like the cops figured it was a dead end, and I guess I agree."

"Guess again!"

"What do you mean?"

"Lewis and I just left from interviewing Craig Mazer again. He says that both Grant and Jack were at the office that night. But Jack wasn't there the whole night. He had come in late— or early, depending on your definition of 2 A.M.—and was engaged in an animated conversation with Grant."

"Hold on. You're telling me that Grant and Jack could have alibied Craig?"

"Yes and no. Grant definitely had a conversation with Craig about some inflated numbers and how to make them go away. But Jack didn't see Craig. Craig was told by Grant not to divulge that he was at the office to protect the business. But as we now know, Grant didn't want anyone to know that he was erasing the security system because of the inflated numbers, and that's why it couldn't be known that he was there."

"Wow! I always thought that Grant was Craig's ally, but he's only looking out for himself and his business."

"Yeah, I know the feeling. When Grant hired me, he seemed so genuine, but as we kept digging, he was and is only looking out for Grant. We think that he hired us to help get Craig out so that there wouldn't be a murder charge against the VP of Dogon Tech. That won't help the initial stock price at the public offering. He doesn't care about Craig actually getting out, only that his business's image would improve."

"But what about the receipts? How did they have those for an alibi?"

"That's something we'll need to check out. You said the name of the bar was Attaboy, right?"

"Yes. But it sounds like you guys are on the right track. I'll keep working on my end from here, but I need to go. I've been on the phone too long."

"Wait! Vanesa, just come back here. We can protect you."

"No, sorry, I have to go." And she abruptly hung up.

CHAPTER 28

HOW COULD WE GET Grant Dogon to admit his lies? This thought played in my mind over and over. Also, how did this connect to the murder of Helen Mazer? I was on my own today, as Lewis had flown to Vermont to check on his team watching Vanesa and get a lay of the land there. As for me, I was trapped in my thoughts. I tried to stop myself from worrying about Vanesa or what she knows, trusting Lewis to handle the situation.

I allowed myself to think about my wife, Lucy, for a moment. She was beautiful and very intelligent. Lucy had worked for a large pharmaceutical company as a chemist. She'd been on the research team for new and upcoming drugs that could potentially help save lives. We had a small group of close couple friends and, of course, Lewis and whomever he was dating at the time. Unfortunately, I hadn't kept in touch with any of them because it was so awkward being in group settings without Lucy. So, they slowly went on with their lives, while mine sat idle. Outside of some of my crazy cases, we had lived an unexciting life. How could any of this have led to her being a target for murder? How did Vanesa know things about my wife's murder? What could I have done to prevent it?

Lucy and I had met in high school. We dated through most of high school, but that was just puppy love. But when she came back from college and got her doctorate here in New York, we rekindled that spark. As soon as she finished school, we were married. We had talked about having kids but were waiting for the right time. I always wondered what our kids would have looked like and what they would be doing now. They wouldn't be that old, but would I be coaching baseball or softball? Would that have changed the outcome?

I pushed hard to put those feelings away. Sometimes I go into a dark place if I go down that rabbit hole. Right now, I must stay focused on Dogon Tech and its leader. We only had two weeks before the company goes public, and I'd like to ruin Grant's perfect day if I can. If that's where the facts lead, that is.

■ ■ ■

Since I was on my own for tonight, I thought I would do some old-school sleuthing. I grabbed some of Grant's money that Cal didn't take and headed out. I figured I was on the job, so why spend my money? I went down to the curb and hailed a taxi. When the cabbie asked where I was headed, I said, "Attaboy. It's a bar off Eldridge Street."

The fare wasn't cheap, but neither was my tip to the driver. Hey, it wasn't my money. I found the metal door with the AB on it and pressed the buzzer. I was allowed entry. The place was a trendy industrial speakeasy, and the prices were upscale. But it was nice and seemed like a cool hangout for a businessperson. I ordered a Manhattan and some empanadas. While I was waiting for my order, I gave the place a once-over. I soon spotted something I was looking for. The point-of-sale system that

Attaboy uses was a Dogon Tech product. Since I knew that Grant and Jack weren't here that night, I was sure they knew how to manipulate the system to print out receipts for that evening. That would mean that the owners were involved, but money talks. I wasn't insinuating that the owners were bad people, but they helped a bad person lie to the police.

When I got my drink, I chatted with the bartender for a while. Her name was Brandy—yes, like the liquor—and she was a wealth of information on the bar. She started working there in 2012 when it went from Milk & Honey to Attaboy. She'd been there since its inception. I figured since she sounded like she was always here, it might be a good idea to ask her some friendly questions. "Hey, Brandy, I heard that Grant Dogon comes to this bar. Is that true?"

"Oh yeah, Grant is a regular. I love it when he comes in because it means that my tip out at the end of the night is going to be really nice. Actually, all the technology in this place was supplied by Grant's company, Dogon Tech. He and the owners have known each other for a long time. Our owner's husband served with him in the military."

"Do you think he'll be here tonight? I sure would like to meet someone as smart as he must be."

"No, he won't be here tonight. He hasn't come in since his company announced that they were going public. He told all of us that we would see him after he got done with the deal, and drinks would be on him!"

"Ah, I see. Well dang, I guess I'll try and come in after that goes down."

I finished my drink and food and left her a Grant-sized tip; it was his money after all. When I left, I searched the streets for any cameras. I didn't see any, but it's dark. I'd have to come back during the daytime hours to check the block more thoroughly.

On the cab ride back, I kept thinking about how smart Grant was, but he sure hadn't covered all his bases. I just asked a simple question and found out that Grant hadn't been at the Attaboy for at least a few weeks. The lies kept piling up, and I was going to find out what's under them.

CHAPTER 29

LEWIS HAD ARRIVED BACK in town early the next morning and called to see if he could come over. "Of course," I told him. I wanted to know how Vanesa was doing and if she was safe.

I put on a pot of coffee and waited for Lewis to arrive. I went through a wave of emotions simply thinking about Vanesa. I really wanted to see her again—just to know she was safe, of course.

When Lewis let himself in, I was pouring myself a cup of coffee. "Would you like some?"

"No, you know I don't like that stuff—gets me all hyper. And you and I both know I don't need to be any more of myself than I already am."

Laughing, I said, "You're right."

"Alright, Angelo, I know you want to know about Vanesa, so I'll run through that real quick, but I have an idea to help get Craig out of holding and off the suspect list entirely."

He ran through the details of Vanesa and where she was. He said the cabin she was in was secluded, and his men had every vantage point covered. He told me she'd picked a great location to hide away because it was really remote. He said she looked healthy but tired. Lewis also said she was always on the phone, but it appeared that she had multiple burner phones, so she was covering her tracks well.

"Thanks, Lewis. It sounds like you have her protected well, and she seems to be doing a good job of protecting herself as well."

I quickly went over what I had found out from Vanesa. "First off, Vanesa informed me that Grant and Jack were the other two people of interest. According to police and receipts, their alibis were good for the time of the murder."

"What receipts? What are you talking about, Angelo?"

"Hold on, Lewis, I'm getting there. Grant and Jack said that they were together at a bar called Attaboy and produced the receipts showing they left at 3 A.M. the night of the murder. Of course, we know that they, in fact, were at Dogon Tech, so while you were gone, I paid a visit to Attaboy. I met Brandy, the bartender, who's been at the bar since it opened. She knows Grant well. She says that he hasn't set foot in there since his company announced they were going public. All the technology in Attaboy is from Dogon Tech. Somehow, they faked the receipts and lied to the police." And then I asked him, "So, what's your plan, Lewis?"

"OK, I hadn't expected that, but it doesn't surprise me that you caught Grant in a lie again. But as for the plan, I was thinking that the only person Grant will admit some truths to is Craig. So, what if Craig were to call him and confront him about not protecting him and saying that he was at work? Those phone calls are recorded and available as a matter of public record. If we can get Mr. Touré to get a copy of that recording of Grant admitting he was at Dogon Tech that night, then he could use it as evidence of his client's story and alibi."

"That's a lot of ifs. And what if Grant knows he's being recorded? He won't say anything incriminating."

"It's worth a shot. I have an idea for Grant knowing as well, to push him to the edge, where he may just slip up. Let me talk to Mr. Touré and see if I can get the phone call set up."

■ ■ ■

We were able to put the phone call plan in motion and even were allowed to be present in another room with a speaker set up to hear both sides of the conversation. We wouldn't be able to use the phone call in court until the recording was released to Mr. Touré, but at least we would know if we had something to get Craig out of this.

Craig dialed Grant's number. The first test would be to see if Grant accepted the charges for the call. Luckily, he did.

"Craig, how are you holding up, buddy?"

"I'm doing OK, Grant, as much as I can be with all of this going on." Craig paused for a few seconds and then said, "Look, Grant, I need your help."

"Anything, Craig. I've been doing everything I can to get you out of there."

"Well, not everything, Grant. You know I was at the office the night of the murder. I was talking to you during the time that they say I killed Helen. You could've been my alibi. I need you to tell them that I was there with you, like I was."

"Craig! We've discussed this. I wasn't in the office that night. I was out discussing the technical problems with the security system over drinks with Jack. I told the police this and have receipts showing we were there. You know that."

"No, Grant, I was at the office, and you were too. We talked about the reports that needed fixing…again."

"Craig, you must have gotten mixed up. That must have been the night before or another night. That night, I wasn't there."

"No, Grant! I will remember that night forever. It's the night that I lost the love of my life, and I would never hurt her! I also remember something else about that night, Grant."

"What, Craig? What else do you think you remember?"

"I remember Jack coming in late that night. He went straight to your office in a mad dash. I couldn't be completely sure it was him until I was leaving. That's when I saw you two having a very heated argument."

"You saw that? I thought you had left already… I mean, that was different, it was a day—"

"Thanks, Grant, that's what I needed to hear. That you know I was there the night my wife was taken away from me."

Craig slammed down the phone, ending the call. He had gotten Grant to admit it. Not in plain English, but he caught him off guard enough to say just enough.

Lewis gazed at me and said, "I knew that if he brought Jack into the conversation, Grant wouldn't be able to react quick enough. It was just enough to push him off balance and say something he'd regret. We got it!"

"Lewis, your plan worked perfectly. Great job. Hopefully it's enough to get Craig out."

CHAPTER 30

MR. TOURÉ WAS ALREADY working on the paperwork known as a Sunshine Request to make the phone call public information and use it as evidence that Craig was where he said he was and could not have killed his wife. Hopefully once the request was granted, he could move for a dismissal.

■ ■ ■

Mr. Touré had worked some magic with the powers that be and was able to get Craig out of jail with all charges dismissed in only two days. Grant had already called and fired us from trying to solve the murder but said that we could keep the briefcase as a parting gift for getting Craig off the hook. But we were still on the case because we had a new client, Mr. Craig Mazer.

Craig obviously still wanted to know who killed his wife, Helen. We told him to not worry about paying us, and we would just put it on Grant's tab. We also wanted a conclusion to this matter.

■ ■ ■

Vanesa had texted me after we had gotten out of the phone call between Grant and Craig. All it said was: *Tell Lewis thank you.*

Apparently, Vanesa doesn't miss much because Lewis said there was no way she would ever see his people, but she did. She figured that they were not there to kill her, or they would have done it already, so she confronted them. They ended up telling her who they worked for, with Lewis's permission, of course, and they would remain there as long as she did.

■ ■ ■

I had spent the last two days idly waiting around for word from Mr. Touré. I had filled my time with thoughts of how to move forward in the investigation, how to help Vanesa, and how to solve Lucy's murder. I really hadn't figured out much of anything. I worked at the bar one night, but the news of Craig getting out wasn't known to the police yet, so they were still fixated on him.

Right now, we needed to focus on Dogon Tech and see where that leads us. It may or may not get us to the final answer, but it's where the trail leads for now. With Craig on board, it may help us navigate around Grant.

Our first meeting with our new client was scheduled today, as Craig wanted to get on it immediately following his release. Lewis and Craig should both be here in an hour. I decided to read the newspaper while I waited, and when I picked it up, I saw the headline, "Craig Mazer Dismissed of All Charges." I read the story for fun—I mean, I know what happened. As I finished reading the story, I noticed a smaller headline that sad, "Related

Story: Head of IT at Dogon Tech Found Dead, Apparent Suicide."

I frantically flipped to the story. There wasn't much there, but it read:

> Cal Dunst, age 23, was found dead late last night by his girlfriend. It was ruled a suicide by the police and coroner. Cal Dunst was the head of the IT Department at Dogon Tech. Story will be updated as more information becomes available.

I felt guilty. If we hadn't approached him or gotten him to give up the secrets he was keeping, he may still be alive. We needed to make sure that we figured this all out or all his help would have been in vain.

I could hear Lewis and Craig out in the hall as they approached and then walked into my apartment. They were both boisterous and full of joy until they saw my face. "What's going on, Angelo?" Lewis asked.

"Have you seen the newspaper today?"

"Yes, of course. Our boy Craig here is front page news, and we even got a shout-out for the firm! Why would that make you look like you do?"

"Not that, Lewis…" I handed him the newspaper turned to the story of Cal. "This."

His face now mirrored mine as he handed it to Craig. After Craig read it, though, he became angry. "This was not suicide! That kid wouldn't have done that to himself!"

"Look, Craig, we're all saddened by this. And you obviously knew him better than we did. For now, we need to deal with it as a suicide unless we find out otherwise. We need to find your wife's murderer. We'll all go to the funeral. He at least deserves that from each of us."

"OK, Angelo. I don't like it and I don't agree, but for now, let's solve my wife's murder."

We rehashed all that we had learned while Craig was in holding and went over a complete retelling of what we knew and any ideas of what else we could do. Craig explained in detail the inner workings of Dogon Tech. He let us know about the security system, where cameras were located, and all the entrances and exits of the building. He told us about Grant's schedule, who he meets with, and what he's doing to get ready for the public sale. For now, Grant didn't know we were pursuing this further, and we wanted to keep it that way for as long as possible.

The first step in our plan was for me to get back to work at the bar, at least for one night, to try and get new information on Helen's murder case now that Craig was no longer a suspect.

CHAPTER 31

I WAS BACK AT the bar as planned. Usually in the middle of big cases, I hardly picked up shifts unless Roy needed me. But tonight, I was working for the case. I needed to hear what the buzz was now that Craig was let go and see if I could get any new information from the police or who they may be pursuing now.

The crowd was light tonight, but they sure were loud and thirsty. That worked in my favor. They knew me and what I do, but loose lips and all that. When I mentioned Craig Mazer, they generally gave me the same answer. It went along the lines of "screw that guy," "he got off on a technicality," and "I still think he did it." I wasn't getting anywhere with these guys.

Then in walked Detective Paul Tanner, the guy who gave me his business card and wanted to help if I needed it and believed Craig was innocent from the beginning. He waved me over to the bar and took a seat at the far end.

As I handed him a beer, he said, "We never had this conversation, and if you ever say we did, I'll deny it. Got it?"

I just nodded. I wanted to hear what he had to say and not interject my opinion or thoughts until he was done.

"I'm in charge of the Helen Mazer murder now. It's been downgraded in urgency since it was long ago—three weeks is a long time for a murder case and its trail. We had two people of interest originally along with Mr. Mazer. They were Grant Dogon and Jack Gaither. They have solid alibis, even though they were said to be together, but there were apparently other witnesses as well. Now that Mr. Mazer got Mr. Dogon on tape saying that Mr. Dogon was actually at the office and that Mr. Gaither came in later, there are holes in their alibis. We're relooking into them both.

"We know that Mrs. Mazer had sex prior to being murdered, and we're now sure that Mr. Mazer was not her partner that night. We're not sure of the motive, but we think whomever she slept with is also her murderer. With that in mind, we've been recanvassing her friends and trying to see if any of them knew more intimate details of Mrs. Mazer's affair. We haven't found that person yet, but she must have talked to someone about it—a best friend or family member. Most people can't hold that kind of secret inside for too long without some kind of an outlet. I'm telling you all of this in hopes that we can help each other and share information. Obviously, it would be on the down-low, but I think we can catch this person together better than we could on our own, especially since you've been working other angles that are not Craig Mazer as the suspect."

"I appreciate it, Detective Tanner. In a normal case, I would need my client's permission to involve the police, but I already know his answer, and it's to find out who killed his wife."

"Wait. You're working for Craig Mazer now?"

"Yes. Mr. Dogon fired us once we got Mr. Mazer out and cleared of the charges. We're working for Mr. Mazer now to find the murderer, and all he cares about is answers. The only information I can share with you that you don't already know is about the security shutdowns. I'm not a hundred percent sure of the why either, so I won't speculate now, but the shutdowns are being done manually by Grant Dogon."

"Wow. How do you know this?"

"Being a police officer, I'm sure you heard about the death of Cal Dunst. He was the head of the IT department at Dogon Tech. Well, he confessed to us a few days ago that he was covering for Grant Dogon because that was his job. Mr. Dogon had told him to make up a story of how the shutdowns were occurring and answer all questions about it with this story. But his conscience got the better of him, and he told me and Lewis all about it."

"Well, that is new information to me. Thank you, Angelo, for trusting me with this information and for being willing to work together. I know that PIs get a bad rap, but I know you're a good one, and you seem to genuinely care. So, I look forward to our future non-meetings."

CHAPTER 32

LAST NIGHT WAS UNEXPECTED. I usually get information from the cops that come into McGinty's, but I've never shared information back. I had a good feeling about Detective Tanner and felt like we could trust him on this one. Also, he was in Craig's corner from the beginning and even risked telling me so.

Today was going to be a full day. Craig was going into the office to "get personal items." Grant had told him to take some time off and to come back to work the day before the company went public to make sure everything was ready to go. But Craig was headed in to get information on Cal's funeral and to see who was running the IT department in Cal's place. Lewis and I were meeting with Detective Tanner, as he said we could sit in on the interviews with the close friends of the Mazers.

We were doing home interviews for two reasons. One, it made people feel more comfortable talking in a normal setting. And second, it would bring less scrutiny of us being there during the interviews.

We first met with Detective Tanner at the home of Jeffery and Dontay Rathmore. They had a nice upscale home in the same community as the Mazers. Detective Tanner introduced us as private investigators working for Craig Mazer but that we were only here as observers. Detective Tanner started by asking the Rathmores how they knew the Mazers.

Dontay started, "Well, all the couples met at the Richmond County Country Club. It was a new member social, and we all happened to be new members around the same time. We hit it off as a group right away and stayed that way for many years."

"It was that way until about the last year or so," Jeffery chimed in.

Detective Tanner asked, "What happened within the last year?"

Jeffery continued, "In the beginning, Helen still came around, but Craig was working all the time. And slowly, Helen drifted off as well, not wanting to be the odd one out. We tried convincing her that we liked having her around still, even without Craig, but it didn't seem to matter."

"Were there problems in their marriage that you knew of?" asked Detective Tanner.

Dontay replied first, "We all have our problems, Detective. But Helen did miss the time that she and Craig used to spend together. They were inseparable until he moved into the vice president role at Dogon Tech."

"OK, I understand Mrs. Rathmore. Now, if we could, we'd like to speak to each of you individually? Let's start with you, Mrs. Rathmore."

They looked a little confused but complied all the same. Mr. Rathmore said they could find him in the garage when they were ready to speak to him.

"Mrs. Rathmore, this part may be more difficult to answer. Was Helen Mazer having an affair? We're only asking because it may be important to the case."

Dontay had a hard time answering. She seemed to be holding back tears when she stated, "Yes, but she never told me who. I only found out about two weeks before she was murdered. She said that she couldn't take the guilt anymore. She was going to stop seeing the other man and tell Craig everything. I hadn't talked to her since then, and now I never will."

She started sobbing, and Detective Tanner stood up to leave her to grieve in peace. But I had to interject, "Mrs. Rathmore, does your husband know about this affair?"

Between sobs, she said, "No, I never told him about it. Helen swore me to secrecy, at least until she talked to Craig. I'm happy that Craig was not the murderer. I just couldn't ever imagine him doing that to her."

Detective Tanner said, while giving me a stern look, "Thank you for your time, Mrs. Rathmore. We'll go out and talk to your husband in the garage and then we'll be on our way."

We headed out without another word to Dontay. As we were leaving, Detective Tanner firmly reminded me that we were only observers. We found Jeffery in the garage not really doing anything. He stood up as we came out.

"What can I answer for you guys?"

Detective Tanner said, "This will be quick, Mr. Rathmore, but may be difficult to answer, and we need the truth. Are you having an affair?"

Jeffery looked stunned and quickly replied, "No! Of course not! What does that have to do with anything?"

"Thank you for your time, Mr. Rathmore. That's all we have for now. I hope that if we need to come back, you'll allow it," Detective Tanner said as he motioned for us to go.

■ ■ ■

We had interviews with both Stan and Judy Bayner and Frank and Heather Hotch. The interviews with them went almost the same as with the Rathmores. The women both had talked to Helen around the same time as Dontay, and neither man admitted to having an affair. Stan did admit to having an affair years ago with one of his assistants, but he and Judy had worked through that, and it was in the past.

After the last interview, we talked through the answers. Each of the women had known of the affair and that Helen was ending it. We wondered if that was why Helen was killed. We also decided that none of the husbands gave any hint of lying or that we were talking about Helen Mazer when asking if they had had an affair.

CHAPTER 33

WHILE DETECTIVE TANNER WAS continuing his pursuit of the killer in his way, we were continuing to look at Dogon Tech for some answers. But for today, that would have to wait. We had a funeral to go to. We didn't know Cal well, but he deserved to have us there.

The church was packed as it usually is when people die so young. He had so much going for him and seemed to be well liked by everyone we talked to. The church service was done beautifully, and many people got up to speak about how Cal Dunst had affected their lives. The last person to speak was his girlfriend. She was the one to find him. She did her best to talk, but she only lasted a few words: "I love you, Cal." Everyone felt the same ripple through the room as she walked back to her pew. It was silent for two minutes until the preacher came back to the altar and dismissed us all.

We decided to go to the burial as well because we were invited. Lewis and I stayed to the back. The crowd was much smaller here. It was mainly family, but Grant, Jack, and Craig were there as well. Craig nodded to us as he passed us, but Grant and Jack wouldn't even look in our direction.

The burial was heart-wrenching. Cal's parents each gave an emotional tribute to their "boy wonder" who had hopes of changing the world. And Cal's girlfriend, who we found out was Nancy, was able to read a poem that she had written for him. It was a powerful tribute to Cal and to her love for him. It went like this:

Life, Love, and Tragedy

We were only just beginning this journey,
A road that had many paths to be discovered.
Our lives crossed at that special point,
When you told me how your life changed
with me in it.
I believed you and took your hand,
Ready to go above and beyond.
My promise to you, now that you're gone,
Is to reach for the sky and truly fly,
And reach those heights destined for two,
Making sure it's in honor of you.
Cal, forever in my heart.

As she read, she stayed strong, but everyone else was crying, including me and Lewis. Her words gave everyone an inside look at the love they shared.

We waited for everyone else to leave before we did. As people passed by, several stopped for handshakes or hugs, even though we had no idea who they were. But when Nancy approached us, she came straight toward me and gave me a huge hug. As she hugged me, she whispered, "Cal told me to give this to you if something happened to him," as she slipped an envelope in my pocket. "I don't know what it is, but I do know Cal didn't kill himself. I wrote my number on the envelope if you need to reach me for any reason at all. Please help Cal with finishing whatever he was involved in."

Then she walked away. Lewis was staring at me quizzically, as if asking, *What was all that about?* I told him, "We'll talk about it later."

We stopped by Cal's casket and dropped some dirt onto the grave. I silently said thank you and sorry. We walked to the car without another word.

CHAPTER 34

IN THE CAR, LEWIS said, "Are you going to tell me what that was all about?"

"I don't know, but…" I held up the envelope, "let's find out. It's from Cal. Nancy said that she was to give it to me if anything happened to him."

"Well, what are you waiting for?"

I tore open the envelope carefully, not knowing what was inside. There was a letter and some key fob thing. I pushed the button on the fob and a number popped up. Lewis and I had no clue what it was, so we decided to read the letter to figure it out.

> *Angelo,*
>
> *I was worried something was going to happen to me, and I guess it has if you're reading this. Grant had found out that I told someone about the glitches. So, I asked Nancy to give this to you because I have some information, maybe. I say maybe because I haven't checked what's on it, but it may prove useful. After Craig was arrested, I put an encrypted USB thumb drive into the back port of the security system server. It has been saving all the recordings since Craig's arrest. Even*

if Grant erased them from the server, it will still be on there. I was going to check it when he erased the system the last time, but I didn't get the chance. I hope there's something on there that will prove useful.

You'll need to get the thumb drive out of the server and plug it into your computer. The thumb drive I installed has a blue dot on it. Once you open the thumb drive files, it will ask you to provide the token key. That's what the fob is for that I've included in the envelope. When it asks for the token key, press the button and a series of numbers will be generated. This is the only way to access what is on the thumb drive.

And Angelo, be careful.

Cal D.

"Cal keeps on providing answers for us, and he's paid the price for it. But how do we get to the thumb drive?" asked Lewis.

We sat and thought about this for a moment. Then we both looked up at the same time and said, "Craig!"

CHAPTER 35

WE CALLED CRAIG AND left him a voice mail to get back to us right away. He was at the funeral reception and probably had his phone turned off. We decided that it could wait until it was over to talk to him. We had done enough to Cal and his family and didn't want to ruin the reception for his loved ones.

The last shutdown of the security system was just over a week ago, the day before we talked to Jack Gaither. He had mentioned the shutdown, not knowing what we knew now. What happened that night? Craig wasn't there, since he was still being held awaiting trial. All the other shutdowns occurred when Craig reported discrepancies, so what did Grant do that night that made him erase everything?

Lewis and I decided that we deserved a drink, and it had been a couple days since we'd seen Roy. It would be nice to go into work and not have to work.

When we got to McGinty's, we got more than we bargained for. Talking to Roy was Grant. As soon as the door opened, he turned and saw us. Grant said, "Oh, hey guys, I was just asking Mr. McGinty very nicely when the next time you worked was. And look, I found you before he could even answer."

Grant was still in his suit from the funeral. I asked him, "What do you want, Grant? And why are you bothering Roy; you know where I live. Also, didn't you fire us?"

"You see, I did, Angelo. And I also told you to stop snooping around my company. Then you turn my friend and vice president of my company against me. You used that taped conversation of us to get him out, and I would have left it alone had you done what I asked after that. But you just couldn't let go. You continue to poke around my company, and I warned you."

"Grant, we're just doing our job and helping Craig find out who killed his wife. Is there something you'd like to tell us to help us with that?" I said snarkily.

"I do have something to tell you: you lost your mole. Craig won't be allowed into the offices anymore. And once this public offering goes through, he'll be fired. So, good job. You got him out but lost him everything else he had."

"OK, Grant, you can leave now. I think you've said all you need to say. I'm glad Craig will be out from under your thumb."

As he started walking out, he said, "I've carried that man since our time serving together. Good riddance."

Lewis got the last word though. "Hey, Grant, I hope you fixed those glitches. Would be a shame if someone found out what they really were before your little sale. Just saying."

"Are you threatening me?"

"No, I'm genuinely concerned for you. I hope that you've fixed all your problems, is all," Lewis said with a dollop of sarcasm.

Grant left fuming. We turned to Roy. "Are you OK?" I asked.

"Of course! He tried intimidating me to tell him your schedule. Heck, I don't even know when you're going to show up for work," Roy said, laughing. "But seriously, guys, he didn't do anything. You came in only a couple minutes after he did."

"OK, Roy, good. Let's share a beer."

CHAPTER 36

CRAIG CALLED US WHILE we were still at McGinty's. We told him to meet us there, and we'd have a beer ready for him. But he said, "Not sure that's a great idea. It's a cop bar, and the cops probably aren't my biggest fans right now."

He was probably right, so we grabbed a six-pack to take back to my apartment to meet him there. Roy laughed as he said, "Thanks for coming to my rescue today, boys!"

■ ■ ■

Craig was waiting for us at the entryway to my apartment. He seemed angry, but we already knew why. Lewis asked, "How was the reception, Craig?"

"Well, the reception was very nice, but what happened at it, not so much."

I said, "Yeah, we know."

"How do you guys know?"

I told him about Grant stopping by the bar and trying to intimidate Roy and then telling us what he had done to Craig. When I had finished the retelling, Craig asked, "What do we do now?"

"We were about to ask you the same thing. Let's go into my apartment. We have something to show you."

When we settled into chairs and each had a beer in hand, we told Craig about Cal and his letter. Craig asked, "How do we get it? I'm not allowed into the building!"

I said, "We know. We thought that was going to be the easy part of this." As I finished saying this, my phone rang. It was Vanesa. "I have to take this. Just a minute, guys."

I stepped into the hallway. "Hey, Vanesa."

"Hey, Angelo. I heard that you got Craig off of the murder charge, and he's free now."

"Yeah, it worked out pretty well. But that can't be why you're calling. Are you OK?"

"You're right, Angelo. I called because we had to change locations. Lewis is probably getting a call from his people right now. There were suspicious vehicles and people getting close to the cabin. And it's not a place that you just happen upon. So, after talking to Lewis's guys, they said they had a safe house they could take me to. I agreed that it was probably the safest option. I'll let Lewis fill you in on where, but I wanted to be the first to tell you what's going on and that I'm safe."

"But, Vanesa, why can't you tell me what you're involved in or what Lucy was involved in? We can help!"

"I promise, Angelo, I'll tell you everything, but for now, just trust me." With that, she ended the call.

When I walked back into the apartment, Lewis and I shared a look and nodded to each other, both aware of what the call was about.

I said, "OK, guys, it's been a long day. How about we meet for lunch tomorrow and go over any ideas anyone gets while sleeping tonight?"

After they left, I finished my beer and reread Cal's letter one more time. Then I slowly drifted off to sleep thinking about Nancy's poem for Cal.

CHAPTER 37

I AWOKE THE NEXT day with no ideas at all on how to gain access to the USB drive. I decided to call Detective Tanner to compare notes. He had been out interviewing neighbors around the Mazers' house the day before. I wanted to see if he had any new information, but I wasn't sure yet if I was going to share mine. I decided to hold back for now, at least until we saw the video.

Detective Tanner shared with me that the neighbors didn't hear anything the night of the murder, but an elderly woman across the street had awoken that night around ten. There was a car in the driveway that she didn't recognize. Unfortunately, all she could say was that it was a four-door sedan. No license plates, color, or make. Other than that, he had no new information from all his canvassing.

I talked to him about Cal's funeral. I told him that Craig, Grant, and Jack were all there. I also told him about Craig effectively being removed from Dogon Tech and no longer able to go into the building.

"Why would he do that?" Detective Tanner asked.

"Well, Craig is working with us, and we're still poking around Dogon Tech. Our working theory is that the murder is somehow connected to them. So, when Grant realized that Craig was working more with us than for Grant, he let him go. Craig won't be officially fired until after the public offering happens. Bad optics to fire your vice president right after his wife was murdered and he was dismissed of all charges. Grant doesn't want anything to affect his bottom line when this sale happens."

"Why doesn't Craig just go to the newspapers and tell them what's happening to him?"

"Because right now the only thing that matters to Craig is justice for his wife. And the more comfortable Grant is, the better our chances are of getting something from him."

■ ■ ■

Craig, Lewis, and I met at Mancini's for lunch. I had nothing to offer on how to get the flash drive, so I just listened. Lewis had come up with a crazy idea of dressing up as janitors and trying to clean the server room after hours. But Craig and I both quickly shot that down.

Craig said, "Look, I have some people I trust still at Dogon Tech and a company that does service checks for the ventilation of the server room. I know a guy from that company who I think will help me out. My plan is to get someone from the office to call in and say the server room temperatures are rising, and that the thermostat doesn't seem to be responding accordingly. They'll call my guy from the service company to fix it. I'll ask him to grab the USB drive from the back of the server while he's in there. I think for the right price, it will go smoothly."

I said, "We have Grant's money still. What do you think it will take?"

"Ten thousand dollars should cover it."

"OK, that sounds like a good plan. Craig, call your people and see if they'll help us out. Lewis, grab the money and bring it to my apartment."

Lewis said, "OK. What are you going to do, Boss?"

"I'm going to make a trip to Dogon Tech. I want to talk to Jack Gaither. I'm not sure if I'll even get past the front desk, but at least they'll know we aren't backing down."

Craig said, "Angelo, be careful. Jack is a dangerous person. I've known him for a long time, and he's quick to act on his instincts, and he doesn't always act rationally. And he is one hundred percent on Grant's side, no matter what. Anything you say to him, he'll run right to Grant and tell him as soon as you leave."

I replied, "Thanks for the warning, Craig, but what I have to say to Jack, I hope he tells Grant."

■ ■ ■

I was right. They wouldn't let me past the front desk. In fact, they told me that I needed to go outside. Even though they wouldn't let me in, Jack did say that he would come down and give me five minutes.

The landscaping was unreal outside of Dogon Tech. They had an elaborate garden with an abundance of greenery. It didn't fit into the streets of New York, but it definitely made a statement, especially with all the glass behind it.

I found a keystone block wall and took a seat. When Jack came out, I wanted him to feel like this was just a conversation, not an interrogation.

Jack finally came out, after making me wait twenty minutes for him. Immediately, he said confrontationally, "What do you want, Barsotti?"

"I only want to talk to you, Jack, or should I call you James?"

He didn't even flinch. "I know you know all about my military life already. I'm Jack now; James is in my past."

"OK, Jack. Can you tell me about your relationship with Craig Mazer? And Helen Mazer?"

"I didn't even know Helen. I may have met her once, but I didn't *know* her. And Craig and I have known each other from back in the military. He has ridden Grant's coattails since then."

"Some would say the same thing about you, Jack."

"I do my thing, and Grant does his. Just because our paths are the same doesn't mean that I ride his coattails. I've done as much for Grant as he has done for me."

"And what have you done lately for Grant, Jack?"

"I don't have any specifics. Just know that I take care of business, whatever that may be."

"I have a specific one for you, Jack. Why are you covering up the fact that Grant has been erasing the security system? The glitches are just a story that was made up, and you're hiding the truth for Grant. What are you two up to?"

It was the first time I knocked the bravado out of him. He opened his mouth to answer several times, but nothing came out. Finally, he said, "I think we're done here. Kindly remove yourself from our property."

He turned around quickly and went straight inside. I saw him motion to security, probably telling them to make sure I leave. Leaving was not a problem. I came and said what I had wanted. I shook Jack up and let both Jack and Grant know that I knew at least one of their secrets, and I was still working to find more, until the case was solved.

CHAPTER 38

THE PLAN WAS PUT in place. We were again back at my apartment going over the details of retrieving the USB drive. It was going to happen tomorrow. Craig's trusted employee on the inside was Lana Wilson.

Lana was one of Craig's first hires when Dogon Tech started. Part of Craig's duties in the beginning was hiring key personnel. He had hired Cal Dunst and Lana Wilson the same day. Cal was in charge, and Lana was second. He had been close to both because, since they were young, he felt like a father figure to them in the business world. They had the smarts, but he knew the business side. So, they all would share teachings with one another. Now that Cal was no longer there, Lana was in charge, but Jack had basically taken over.

Lana said that Jack had a routine, and that every morning he would leave for about an hour to meet with Grant. It was at ten o'clock sharp on most days, so that's when the service call would be set up for.

The service call was arranged with Wesley Hanover, the owner of Serving Servers. They're a service company that helps maintain servers in large companies. Wesley had met Craig the day that Dogon Tech had hired his company to provide his services. They had become friends over time. They would share stories about their wives, golf trips, and good food.

Craig said that he explained to them the extent of their service was to help him recover something important that he had left there, and since he was not allowed back in the building, he needed their help. Both had their reservations but trusted Craig enough to do it for him. The money helped clear their consciences as well.

We all agreed that the plan should be easy to accomplish, but we should have contingencies in place. *What if Jack doesn't go to his meeting?* Craig said that Wesley was ready to move as soon as Lana called. *What if they can't find it?* Craig said that Wesley knew the servers inside and out, and he would notice something that doesn't belong. *What if they decide to turn over the USB to Jack?* I said, "Then we were sunk before we started. We trust Craig, and he trusts them, so hopefully it runs as smooth as we think it should."

CHAPTER 39

THE WAITING PERIOD HAD begun. The three of us were sitting in Katz's Deli. Luckily, they opened early because we got there around 9:30 A.M. We wanted to be near Dogon Tech when Wesley got the USB. We didn't want it to go far before we got our hands on it.

The mood was tense, so conversation was kept to a minimum. We had each gotten the loaded omelet with pastrami, but it seemed that none of us had much of an appetite.

We sat there staring at nothing or each other for a while. By 11 a.m., we had expected to hear something, but Wesley hadn't even called to tell us he was on his way. But then at 11:30, the plan was a go. Wesley texted that he was headed up.

We all let out a sigh of relief that the plan was in motion. But now, there was a nervous excitement and a little bit of fear. This next part of waiting was going to be even worse because we had now involved more people in crossing Grant Dogon and Jack Gaither. Hopefully there was nothing to worry about.

■ ■ ■

It was an excruciating two hours. This was supposed to be a quick in and out with Wesley fixing the overheating with a quick push of some buttons and an inspection of the servers. Finally, he called and said he was on his way over. We waited for him outside of the deli.

When Wesley approached, I couldn't help myself when I blurted out, "What happened? What took so long? Did you get it?"

Wesley said, "When I got up to the IT department, Lana was waiting. I went to correct the 'problem' and then told them that I was going to check things out in the server room to make sure nothing was disturbed by the issue. I got the USB drive—easy to find when you knew what to look for. But when I came back out, Jack Gaither was there. He grilled me for a while about why I was there and who had called. I told him Lana had called and since I happened to be nearby, I thought I'd stop by and quickly fix the issue. That didn't sit completely right with Jack, so then he questioned what I was doing in the server room. Unfortunately, he saw that I had dropped a USB drive into my pocket. I was going to show Lana that I had gotten it but tried to quickly slip it into my pocket when I saw Mr. Gaither. He asked for me to give him the drive that I had put in my pocket and asked what was on it. I said I didn't know, that when I was checking out the servers I noticed it, and it shouldn't have been there. He made me hand over the drive and told me that while he appreciates me fixing the system and looking out for Dogon Tech, that nothing that is Dogon Tech property should ever leave the building unless authorized. I apologized and said that the service call was on the house, and then I left."

"Shit!" all three of us said in unison.

I then asked, already knowing the answer, "So, Jack has the USB drive?"

Wesley said, "He has *a* USB drive."

"What does that mean, Wesley?" Lewis asked.

"Well, I came prepared. When I dropped the one with the blue dot into my pocket, I pulled out another one that I had brought with me, just in case."

Wesley stood looking very proud of himself until I finally realized, "Wait…you have the USB that Cal left for us?"

"Yes! I gave Mr. Gaither a drive that's been completely wiped and is untraceable to anyone or anything."

"You're a genius! Thank you so much, Wesley! Can we see it?" I asked like a little kid who was about to get a Christmas gift.

"Of course." Wesley pulled out a thumb drive with a blue dot on it, just as Cal had described in his letter. "Here ya go."

As he handed me the drive, Lewis handed him an envelope. Craig patted Wesley on the back and thanked him. I hugged him for his brilliance and said thank you as well. Then Wesley departed, heading back to his van.

CHAPTER 40

WE IMMEDIATELY HEADED TO my apartment. On the way back, we couldn't believe what had happened and how Wesley had gotten out of there with the drive. I asked Craig if he had thought of bringing the extra USB, and he said that it was all Wesley.

We ran into the apartment and stuck the USB drive into the port. It took a few seconds to load up. I clicked on the video file to open it. When I did, a pop-up came onto the screen. It said:

Please activate your token to open the file and enter number sequence below. Once it's entered, click Open to proceed.

I pressed the button on the token, and it read: *87738902123*. I entered the code, clicked Open, and the video file started opening.

It was a large file, and it said the download time was 1 hour and 53 minutes. So, we had some more waiting to do. It was another stare fest, this time at the counter ticking down on the screen.

Finally, the file opened. There were twelve days' worth of video. When you opened a day's video, twenty miniature screens filled the main screen. When you click on one of them, it opens to just that screen. We knew what day we were looking for but not which screen we needed to watch on that day. Something happened during the eighth shutdown, the day before we met with Jack Gaither at Dogon Tech, and Grant had erased it for some reason.

We decided that the best way to not miss anything was to open each screen and fast-forward through the twenty-four-hour period looking for Grant in each one. We figured that if he was the one who erased the security, then he must have been involved.

We searched through seven screens, making notes on each one Grant had been in. Yet, so far, nothing had jumped out at us as to the reason for the shutdown. It was late, and we were losing concentration. We didn't want to stop, but we had to. If we missed something important because we were tired, then it would have all been for nothing.

Since we wanted to start back on this first thing, Lewis and Craig slept on the couches. First one up would wake the others.

■　■　■

At 6 A.M., I was the first one up. I started some coffee and woke up Lewis and Craig. We opened the video file, having to go through the token sequence again, but at least it was already downloaded. We clicked on the eighth screen. This one was Grant's office.

We fast-forwarded through most of the day. He was hardly in his office, and it wasn't until near the end that we saw it.

Around ten that evening, Detective Tanner walked into Grant's office. When Detective Tanner entered, Grant, who was sitting at his desk, reached into one of his desk drawers. He pulled out something wrapped in a bag. Detective Tanner looked suspiciously at Grant.

"Where's the audio? Turn it up!" I shouted. "Craig, do these recordings have sound?"

"Yes, they usually do. I'm not sure why there isn't any audio."

We tried everything we could think of to get the audio working but to no avail. We were going to have to bring someone else in on this. Lewis said he had a guy who could help, but he wouldn't be able to get him here until tomorrow. After thinking it through, I said go ahead and get him here.

We decided to watch the rest of the video. After Grant put the bag back into the drawer, he began talking. Tanner responded. They went back and forth, with Tanner getting more and more animated, while Grant seemed to be completely under control. Eventually, they shared a look and Detective Tanner left, looking defeated. After he left, Grant made a phone call. When he finished his call, he opened his computer and did something on it. Then he left. We continued watching, but nothing else happened the rest of the night that we noticed.

We spend the rest of the day watching the rest of the camera feeds. There was nothing on them with Grant at all, except for the parking lot feed, where we saw him leaving with the bag in his hand.

CHAPTER 41

AFTER THE LONG DAY and night, I decided to sleep in. I had sent Craig and Lewis home last night; they needed a shower and a proper night's sleep. Lewis's friend Keith Brinker was due in this afternoon from California. Craig was going to meet me here, and Lewis was coming to get us.

I sat and rewatched the video exchange between Grant and Tanner four times, trying to get anything out of it. But it was the same thing over and over. I couldn't stand it. We were so close, but again, here we were waiting.

I do this sometimes—actually, I do it a lot. When I can't figure something out, I overanalyze. I look for things that aren't there. It's the same reason that I reread the same news article about Lucy's murder. I'm hard on myself when I fail. I know that it may be irrational at times, that some things are out of my control, but I don't like it. I like to be in control, and right now, I wasn't feeling in control of anything in my life. Lucy, Vanesa, Craig, Helen, Grant, Jack, and even this video. Lewis was the only constant in my life, and he was the only reason I stayed grounded.

Lewis texted that he and Craig were waiting outside. I glanced at the clock. I had just wasted three hours in my own head.

When I get outside to meet the guys, they look refreshed and ready for the day. I, on the other hand, was still in a fog. Lewis noticed and said, "Hey, Angelo, let's go! Keith will be waiting for us! We have a big day ahead of us."

I snapped out of it, and we headed to the airport. Keith was waiting for us at the curb. I immediately noticed that he didn't look like your typical tech guy. He looked more like a lumberjack bodybuilder. This large, muscular man gave Lewis a huge bear hug and then introduced himself to us with a crushing handshake.

We piled into the car. What had been a comfortable ride was now a tight squeeze. Keith started asking questions right away. "What do we have, guys? Lewis told me that you have a video file, but the audio isn't there. I know there must be more to it than that because Lewis sent a first-class ticket for me to get here as soon as possible."

I said, "We have an issue with a video file that was recorded from a security system. The security footage usually has audio with it. We can't seem to pull the audio from anywhere, so we need your help. Lewis only calls in the best, so you must be the best."

Keith replied, "Well, I appreciate that, and I'll try to get the audio for you. The best thing for me to do is to get my eyes on it."

I said to Keith, "We'll take you right to the file. This is a very sensitive case, and someone was murdered. Actually, it was Craig's wife. We've already gotten him out of jail, and now we're trying to solve who did kill her. This file could be a big break in our case. I don't think I need to tell you this, but this will be confidential, correct?"

Keith and Lewis shared a laugh. "Angelo, I'm a professional hacker. I've worked for the government, private companies, and everything in between. Confidentiality will not be a problem."

"I appreciate your help, Keith."

■ ■ ■

I opened the file using the token so that Keith could start trying to do whatever it is that he was going to do. He asked us if there was a specific part that we needed audio on, since it was a large file, and even though he may be able to do it, it would take longer for the whole thing. So, I set up the video to the incident in Grant's office with Detective Tanner and showed him that we wanted the audio up until he leaves the office and after Grant's phone call.

Keith talked us through each step as he was doing it. "OK, since this is the part you most need to get audio from, I'm going to extract this segment and isolate it. Then I'm going to run my software, the software I created, to run a diagnostic on it. Basically, once it's done, it will at least tell me if there is an audio file to find or if you flew me out here for nothing because this video never contained audio. But we'll have an answer of some kind."

He continued, "Alright, it's running the check. It's going to take some time. Can we go get some lunch? It's been a couple years since I've been to New York."

Here we go again. I suggested, "How about just you and Lewis go? Catch up. I'm not hungry and am feeling anxious for this to be done."

Lewis said, "Sure thing, Boss. Craig, you want to join us?"

Craig regarded me, trying to discern if I wanted him to stay or go. I spoke up for him, "Yeah, Craig. Sorry, didn't mean to leave you out. Grab a bite and tell Keith about what's going on and your whole situation. Fill him in on all the details."

Craig said, "Sounds good. I was starving."

Keith looked back at me and said, "Hey, let us know when the scan finishes."

"Sure thing, but...how will I know when it's done?"

He pointed to the computer screen and said, "See this box right here, with the moving bars? When it's done, it will say 'Scan Complete.' That's how you'll know."

"Got it. Enjoy some New York food. And thanks for coming. I'm just exhausted."

CHAPTER 42

I DIDN'T WANT TO go out because I needed some alone time. The last few days have been like college with roommates all over again, always having someone around. I needed to decompress and regain my focus. I felt like we were getting close to the final push, and I needed to be at my best.

I started with some breathing exercises and some light meditation. When I felt calm enough and my breathing was at a constant, I began a deeper meditation to control my heart rate and get into a zen state. I awoke, not from sleep, but from an elevated state of mind. I was relaxed and ready to go. And so was the video: "Scan Complete."

I sent Lewis a text:

Get back here now. Scan complete.

■ ■ ■

They came into the apartment looking relaxed and satisfied. I felt the same. They needed food and company, while I needed peace and quiet. Keith headed straight for the computer.

"It's here!" he shouted. He then tried to open the audio file and the token key box popped up. I found the token and pressed the button: *76390261534*. He entered the key and the audio file opened.

"OK, now I just need to merge these files together so that they will play on top of each other as they were meant to. It was simply separated when he encrypted the files."

I asked with a bit of dread, "How much longer will that take? How much longer will we need to wait? I know it's not you, and this isn't your fault, but all we have doing is waiting and—"

Interrupting, Keith said, "Done! Would you like to watch it?"

"Of course! Hit play!" I said excitedly.

We all huddled around the computer. Keith gave us some space. I hit play and we watched the following exchange:

Detective Tanner walks into Grant's office. Grant leans down and pulls something wrapped in a bag from the desk drawer. Tanner looks suspiciously at Grant.

Grant puts it back into the drawer. He says, "What I have here is the evidence you need to solve the Helen Mazer murder. But you can't have it yet."

Detective Tanner says, "Why won't you just give it to me now? Why did you call me over here during my off hours to show me this if you aren't going to give it to me? I could have you arrested for obstruction."

"I know that you could arrest me, but I have an offer for you. I need this to not be solved until the public offering happens. So, for my part of the deal, I will put one hundred shares of Dogon Tech in your name, and when the sale happens, they will be worth millions. You'd have money and still solve the murder, just on my timeline. All you need to do is wait, and I'll help you solve the case."

"So, if I wait for you to make your company public, you'll turn over the evidence?"

"Yes, and I'll make you very rich. Call it your retirement plan."

Detective Tanner looks like he is wavering, fighting the urge to go against everything he believed in. Finally, he says, "Deal." He hangs his head, defeated, as he walks out.

Grant picks up the phone. After a couple of seconds, he begins talking. We could only hear his side of the conversation.

"Detective Tanner just left."

"Yes, he agreed to the plan."

"No, I'm not going to turn you in, or the evidence."

"He'll get his money, and I'll use it to hang over his head if he ever tries to come against us. It's my turn to protect you."

CHAPTER 43

WHAT DID WE JUST watch? How could Detective Tanner have gone along with this? I trusted him! And who was Grant talking to? Obviously the killer, but who? Everyone was staring at me, waiting for me to say something about what we'd witnessed. I was at a loss for words; I could barely keep a thought straight.

Keith broke the silence, "Hey, guys, the tension seems to be pretty high. Who wants a drink?"

"I need a few!" I answered.

Lewis said, "Let's go to my place. I'll call a bartender, and we can hash all this out while drinking whatever you'd like."

"Sounds like a great plan," I said, and everyone agreed.

■ ■ ■

We pulled up to Lewis's place. Every time I came here, I felt like I was stepping into a movie. Lewis lived on the 34th floor of the VU, a thirty-six-story residential high rise in midtown Manhattan. His penthouse condo took up the entire floor, as he bought both duplexes and converted it into one suite. There's a doorman in a suit and tie and a front desk person who knows every resident. Everything inside is immaculate, like it had been cleaned right before we came in. The marble floors sparkle, and all the wood finishes make it look brand new.

Lewis swiped his key card on the elevator so that it would take us to his floor. The elevator opened straight into his condo, and the size of the place is overwhelming. Lewis has a butler, a maid, and a chef. He also has drivers on call and, apparently, bartenders on call as well. A man in a tuxedo greeted us with a tray of tequila shots and said, "I'm Francisco, and I will be your bartender for the evening. I've chilled Clase Azul tequila shots to get you started. The bar is right over there when you're ready for any type of drink you'd like. Also, snacks are set up on the terrace if you're hungry, and there's water to keep you hydrated for the evening."

Each of us grabbed a shot glass, raised them, and said cheers. Then we headed out to the terrace to discuss the video. Keith and Lewis stopped by the bar first and got started on their second round of drinks.

I had finally gathered my thoughts, with the shot of tequila helping to settle my mind. I said, "Let's start with the facts. Grant knows who killed Helen. Detective Tanner is making money by holding the case up until the public offering. And lastly, Grant is planning on not turning over the evidence he says he has once the sale is done. Did I hit everything?"

Craig said, "That about sums it up. Grant could have saved me from the start by turning in whoever did it. But he turned his back on me and on Helen. I can't believe this man has been part of my life for so long and could do that to me."

Lewis summoned Francisco, who he appeared with another tray of tequila. We raised our glasses, and Lewis said, "To Helen."

We all repeated, "To Helen."

I pressed on. "We now know that we can't trust Detective Tanner. He was on your side genuinely at first, Craig, but every time I've met or talked to him since, he's been against us figuring this out, at least before Grant's timeline."

Lewis spoke up, "Craig, who could Grant be protecting? Do you have some idea at least?"

"Grant owes a lot of people favors. So, the list is longer than I want to guess at right now. Let me think it over. Let's get another round."

As if Francisco were listening, he appeared with another tray of tequila. Apparently, this night was not going to be a strategy session. I understood that Craig was upset to learn that the person closest to him had betrayed him. Not only had Grant left Craig in jail, but he also wouldn't turn in the person who killed his wife.

We raised the glasses once again. It was Craig's turn to propose the toast: "To the friends we didn't know we needed, and to the friends we probably shouldn't keep."

We all followed up with, "Cheers."

It turned into a long night, so we all stayed at Lewis's. He had enough rooms for each of us to have our own room. The plan was to get back on track with a brunch prepared by his chef in the morning.

CHAPTER 44

BRUNCH WAS SITTING ON the table when we all stumbled out of our rooms. There was so much food. I counted twelve different entrees, and there were only four of us. But the smells…the smells took me to another planet. We sat down and started in on the amazing meal that Lewis's chef had prepared.

I was feeling a little better than when I woke up. With some food in my stomach, I was ready to get started. Keith had to catch his flight home, so we said our goodbyes and thanked him for his help. He asked that we let him know how it all turned out, and he offered to be on the next flight if we needed any more help.

We went out to the terrace with our waters. We needed to figure out how to get Grant to tell us who had killed Helen. We already knew he was going to double-cross Detective Tanner, so waiting for the sale to happen wouldn't matter. And it would make me feel better if Grant didn't get the satisfaction of the sale going well before he went down.

"Craig, I know last night was crazy, but did you have a chance to think of a short list of people that Grant could be protecting?" I asked.

"Actually, that's what I spent brunch thinking about. Because it seems that Grant is protecting the business by protecting the killer, it must be someone who works at Dogon. The only people I can think of that Grant would care to protect would be someone that served with us. There are four guys from our platoon that work at Dogon, including myself. The other three are Jack, Brock Jensen, and Jonathan Cooper."

Lewis asked, "OK, can you give us a brief overview of each?"

"Yes. Jack, or James, was discharged from the army while we were serving for attempting to steal government technology. He doesn't have a significant other that I know of. Brock joined our platoon late but fit right in. He's the youngest of the group but has two kids and a wife. Jonathan was with us from the beginning. He lost a leg during a routine perimeter check that he and Grant were doing. But Grant said that if Jonathan hadn't thrown him away from the land mine, Grant would have died. He's married with no kids. And I was second in command of our platoon. I always had Grant's back, whether he was right or wrong. I was married but now am widowed."

Craig took a minute, collected himself, and continued, "Grant was our leader. We always protected one another. Jack and I were definitely closer to Grant than the other two. Jack and I butted heads a lot. He hated when I became vice president, but he always knew it was coming. Brock and Jonathan are high-level team leaders and are paid better than the other team leaders we have. I know both of them well.

"As much as it pains me to even think about it, because it means that one of them was having an affair with my wife, I think we should pursue the team."

"I appreciate your thoughts and information. We can't mess this up—not for you and not for Helen. We need to pursue all three without any preconceived opinions. Lewis, get your people researching all of them, please. Craig, I want you to call Brock and Jonathan and ask if we can meet with them. Also, give me a description of Brock and Jonathan, please. I'm going to head back to my place and review the video to see what all three were up to in the past week."

Craig said, "Brock is younger than us, with a head full of curly blond hair. He sits across from Jonathan. Jonathan has a prosthetic leg and walks with a small limp. He has brown hair in a buzz cut."

"Thanks, Craig. I should be able to figure out who they are from that. Please don't let them know that they are possible suspects; just say you need their help in solving the case."

CHAPTER 45

I BEGAN LOOKING THROUGH the video feeds one by one again. Keith left his software for us because he thought if we found anything else, we could duplicate how he showed us step-by-step what he originally did to integrate the audio and video of Grant and Tanner's meeting. He also said we could call and he would walk us through the process again if needed, which we probably would.

I started with Brock Jensen. I went through all the video feeds. He does the same thing over and over, day in and day out. He meets with his team, works at his desk, chats with Jonathan, and then leaves.

Jonathan Cooper wasn't much different. He has the same tasks and meetings like Brock, but he socialized more with others. He didn't seem to do much work—more of a person who goes around talking with everyone. But still, no red flags.

Jack Gaither had a higher role than the other two. But his main purpose throughout the videos was to watch over the IT department. He had daily meetings with Grant and no one else. I separated those meetings out into isolated segments and started running the software Keith had left. Due to the length of the segments all put together, it said it would take approximately four hours to run through the program.

While I was waiting for the program to find the audio files, Lewis and Craig showed up. Craig said that we could meet with Brock and Jonathan tonight after dinner. Lewis didn't have anything new yet on the suspects.

"We need to find a way to talk to Jack without Grant around. And we need to talk to Grant," I said to them.

"But how?" Lewis asked. "Grant has warned us to stay away, and Jack is his lap dog."

"Jack should be easy to get to but hard to get to talk," Craig said. "Leave Jack to me. I'll get him to have a sit-down with you."

Then Craig left. Lewis looked at me and asked, "What are you going to do, Angelo? Even if you get Grant to agree to meet with you, are you just going to say, 'I know you know who killed Helen, tell me!' and he's going to tell you?"

"Obviously not, Lewis. I need you to find something on Grant that we can use, anything at all. I've found the meetings between Jack and Grant and am using Keith's program to get the audio. They may be all about work, but maybe not. Unfortunately, the program won't be finished for a couple hours. I'll review them and see if there's anything we can use. Then we'll talk to Brock and Jonathan tonight."

"OK, Angelo, I agree. We need something on Grant, but it needs to be something of value for him to tell us anything. It has to hurt him or his company. Let me know what those videos have on them, and I'll see you tonight."

■ ■ ■

I caught myself staring blankly at the screen. Then my phone rang. "Hey, Vanesa, how was the move?"

"Everything is quiet right now. But I need to talk to you about Grant and Jack, formerly James. I called one of my contacts in the military. He's an MP—Military Police—who knows about James Grayson's dishonorable discharge. He pulled the files for me and went over them. James was charged with trying to steal government technology. He was asked over and over who was involved with the scheme to get the technology, but James said it was him and him alone. They didn't have any real evidence but knew he was at least part of it, so they discharged him with no further punishment. His contact said that in the notes, though, there was a handwritten sentence: *Grant Dogon is involved.* There was no formal investigation into Grant, but they believed he played a part as well. Also, Grant's first company he sold to the government was weapons technology. I think Grant did get the technology and used it to develop his system. And James took the fall to protect Grant. My contact agrees, and off the record, he thinks that the government let Grant take it while his buddy James was used to take the fall."

"Wow, Vanesa, that's very interesting, and it might be what we need to push a wedge between Grant and Jack. We've found out that Grant knows who the killer is and is using the sale of his company to bribe at least one detective on not pursuing the case as fast as he should be."

"Looks like we're both going in the right direction. But I need to go, Angelo."

"Wait, Vanesa, when are you coming home? When can we talk about what's going on with you?"

"Soon, Angelo." She hung up just as the program got finished finding the audio files.

CHAPTER 46

UNFORTUNATELY, I WASTED A lot of time with the meetings between Grant and Jack. It was all business every time, with one exception. In one video, Jack confronted Grant during one of their meetings about continuing to erase the security system. He was telling Grant that they needed to not have any more issues or it could affect the stock price. Grant said that the last one would be the last time. But that was all I found. At least now we knew that Jack knew the whole scheme. But with the info from Vanesa and hopefully anything Lewis could find, hopefully we would be able to get to the two of them.

It was time to meet with Brock and Jonathan. We were meeting Brock first at a bar in his neighborhood. We found him at the back of the bar. He was wearing jeans, a T-shirt, and a trucker hat with those blond curls spilling out everywhere. He looked like he kept himself in great shape, something I had noticed while reviewing the videos. He stood up to give Craig a big hug and his condolences and then shook both of our hands. He had a firm handshake and a confidence about him. We all sat around the table, where Brock had already ordered a bucket of beer for us.

Our conversation with Brock was simple. He was a homebody and home most nights by six. He didn't go out very often. He said he was home the night of the murder and that his wife and kids could vouch for him if he needed them to. We didn't. This was not our guy. Assumptions were not usually made that quickly, but we could just tell.

But I did want to ask him about something else. "Brock, what happened with James Grayson, or Jack as he's known now, when he was discharged? Did Grant have something to do with that?"

"Look, guys, I've answered your questions about Craig's wife, and I don't really have anything to say other than what I've already told you. I'm going to head home now. Craig, again, I'm deeply sorry for your loss, and I hope you can figure this out."

With that, he left. Craig looked at me and asked, "What was that about? What does that have to do with this?"

"Well, Craig, since you're asking, can you give me your answer on what happened the night that James was discharged for?"

"First off, these guys, Brock and Jonathan, will not say a word about that night. They're loyal to Grant and our code to protect each other. Grant has broken that code for me, so I'll tell you, but these guys won't. So, that night, Grant had a plan to steal technology from the government. Where we were stationed, they had a brand-new geo tracking system. Grant figured that if he could get that technology, he would be able to add it to the homing missile he was planning on developing when we got out. James took it upon himself to get Grant the technology, to prove that he should be number two to Grant. They caught James, and he denied anyone else being involved. He took the fall for Grant and didn't hang his commander out to dry. But the crazy thing is, Grant ended up with that technology anyways. He never told me how, but it was the same geo tracking system he used in developing the homing missile system he sold to the government."

■ ■ ■

We met up with Jonathan, but it was close to the same story as Brock. He was home with his wife and doesn't really go out unless he's with his wife. I didn't even ask about James's discharge. Our focus was now on breaking Jack and Grant. Jack must be involved somehow, and we already knew Grant was involved. Either one could be our killer. I knew Craig thought that Grant was at the office the whole time he was, but what if he wasn't?

CHAPTER 47

CRAIG HAD GOTTEN JACK to agree to meet up with him. Jack didn't know we would be there, but we would be. Craig told Jack he needed a friend to lean on, and Jack couldn't turn his back on him. They were meeting at Attaboy. The plan was for me and Lewis to show up five minutes after Craig joined Jack.

When we walked into Attaboy, I noticed Brandy was at the bar. I stopped by to say hello. She remembered me, or at least pretended to. We could see Jack and Craig at a back table, with Jack's back to us. We had told Craig to make sure Jack's back was to the door so he wouldn't see us approach.

We quietly grabbed two chairs and sat at their table. "Funny running into you two here," I said.

Jack glanced our way and shook his head. "I'm not supposed to talk to you two. Craig, did you set me up?"

Craig said, "Look, Jack, we're just trying to figure out who killed Helen. And you're on our suspect list. So, we can stay here and talk like civilized people, or we can try some different tactics."

"I'm not going to say anything, especially to you, Craig. We used to be close, and as soon as Grant became our platoon leader, you bailed on me. Then you let me take the fall by myself on that one thing—you know what I'm talking about. And you've treated me like a charity case since you hired me." Jack was rambling, so we let him talk.

"I'm the glue that holds this group together. I make things happen that no one else is willing to do. Don't you see that, Craig? I need to go. I shouldn't be here. If Grant knew, he'd kill me."

Jack got up and left without looking back. I returned my gaze to Craig. "Craig, what was he going on about?"

Craig looked saddened and angry. He said, "He's right about some things. He always would do the things we didn't want to—some things I can't even talk about. But it was always for Grant. Grant is the center of this, and we need to talk to him. And we need him to *talk*."

CHAPTER 48

THE FOLLOWING DAY, I had Lewis come over. We needed to get this done. The public offering for Dogon Tech was in three days, and we didn't want Grant to get away with covering up any of this. And if he was the killer, we didn't want him to have extra money to run either. Sure, he could run now, but he wouldn't get the deal done with Dogon Tech. And Grant was too confident to run. He thought he had everything taken care of.

Lewis came up with a plan to get Grant to talk to us, with another ambush. Lewis was going to try and convince one of his wealthy friends to set up a meeting with Grant to try and purchase Dogon Tech before the public offering. It happens all the time, so Grant wouldn't flinch at the offer.

Lewis called on Julie Greenwald. She was the first person to start a cryptocurrency exchange platform. She owned multiple businesses and was buying all the time. Lewis told her enough to convince her to help us, and she even offered up her conference room for the meeting.

■ ■ ■

We arrived at the Green Exchange offices. The building was modernized on the inside. The nice touch about these offices, though, was the number of plants everywhere. They were really playing off her company name. Julie was waiting for us at the front desk. She was a petite woman, probably in her late twenties. She had a streak of purple in her hair and looked like she could handle herself in any situation. She was neatly dressed in a business skirt and a colorful blouse. She was part of the new world, and we simply existed in it.

She handed us our visitor passes and gave Lewis a hug. Lewis said, "This is Angelo Barsotti, my best friend and private investigator."

She said, "Nice to meet you. Lewis has filled me in on the situation, and I'm happy to help."

"Nice to meet you as well, and I really appreciate it. How do you know Lewis?"

She smiled and gave Lewis's arm a squeeze before answering, "Lewis and my dad are friends. They run charity functions and everything that goes with them to raise money for this and that. So, when I had my idea to start the crypto exchange, Lewis was my first investor. I wasn't even pitching it to him; I was talking to my dad. Lewis stood up and wrote me a check right there for fifty percent of the startup expenses."

Lewis said, "She had a great business plan, and I was investing in her more than the idea. But I'm sure glad I did because she has made more money back than I could have ever asked for."

She took us up to the 14th floor and into her conference room. We started going over the numbers. Julie had pulled some reports on what the expected price would be for the public offering of Dogon Tech. She had the expected number of shares to be offered and price per share. To pull this off, she would need to offer something well over those numbers for Grant to even entertain a meeting. Julie showed us the number that was realistic but enough to make Grant want to meet. Then she made the call to Grant.

After a few minutes of discussion—from what we could hear on our end about why she wanted to buy—they agreed to a meeting. Grant agreed to meet her at her offices the next day, but he would be bringing his accountant and financial advisor.

"We needed Grant alone," I said, a little more agitated than I meant to sound.

"I understand, but he was adamant that he has his team here, or he wouldn't come. I thought it would be better to at least get him here," Julie said.

"You're right. I'm sorry. Thank you for that. We'll just need to separate them somehow."

CHAPTER 49

LEWIS AND I WERE at the Green Exchange by eight the next morning. The meeting wasn't until eleven, but we wanted to be prepared, trying to prevent any surprises. We went over the plan with Julie. She was going to meet with Grant and his team and talk about the sale. She was going to make a big pitch and get him all excited. Then she would excuse herself to go to the restroom. Next, she would come back in and ask Grant's team to meet with her team in their financial office. This was her idea to get them separated. If Grant asked to go too, she would ask that he stay so that she could talk to him privately. If all went to plan, the second time she would come out with his team, and we would enter.

Craig joined us at nine. He was meeting with Julie's financial team to prepare them with a sales pitch that would keep Grant's team occupied while the three of us had a little chat with Grant.

By 11 A.M., the three of us were hiding out in Julie's office. Her secretary let us know that everyone was in the conference room. Julie thought that the pitch would last approximately twenty minutes before she would excuse herself, but it took thirty. She came into the office and said, "Grant wants to get this done today. I should be able to get his team out easily because of his eagerness and his willingness to do whatever it takes to get it done today. So, get ready, guys. Give me about five more minutes."

Five minutes later, her secretary came into the office and said, "Mr. Dogon is alone in the conference room."

We rushed straight over. Craig wanted to walk in first to see the dumb look on Grant's face when he realized that he was being set up. And we got it.

Grant sat there, frozen and speechless for a full thirty seconds, until eventually he said, "What in the hell are you three doing here? I told you to stay away from my business, and I'm in the middle of an important meeting."

Craig said, "No, Grant, you're not. The meeting is fake. Julie Greenwald does not want to buy your company. We needed to talk to you, and this was the only way."

Grant said, "I have nothing to tell you."

I said, "Well maybe we should start by telling you. We can tell you what we know and see if your feelings change."

Grant scanned the room. He started fidgeting and seemed completely out of his element. Grant was used to being in control, and right now, we had control.

He then sat up in his chair, chest puffed out, and defiantly said, "Sure, let's see what you've got. This should be fun."

"You're right, Grant, this should be fun," I said. "Let's start with bribery. We know that you promised Detective Tanner one hundred shares in stock when you sell. You traded to him the fact that you know who murdered Helen Mazer for his agreement to slow down the process of solving her murder. But after the sale, you would turn over evidence that would give him the killer's identity."

"I knew that cop couldn't keep his mouth shut," Grant said, breaking his cool a bit. "All he had to do was wait, and I would've given him millions and the case on a silver platter."

"Wrong again, Grant," Lewis said, jumping into the conversation. "We also know that you have no intention of turning over your so-called evidence. We also know that you were going to use that payoff to blackmail Detective Tanner."

"That's a lie. I told him I would hand over the evidence after the public sale." Grant wasn't sounding so confident anymore.

Craig got in on the action too. "What about James? Did you involve him in this? I know that you've pushed him too far before. Remember the night of the security heist in the military, Grant? You told all of us your grand plan to get the technology and then sent James in alone. You made him think it was his idea, but you pushed him to it. I heard all of it. I never told you because we were a team and you were our leader. When James was discharged, I thought you may do something to get him out, but you got what you wanted and that's all that mattered. He got the technology for you, didn't he? And then he got caught, and you let him take the fall by himself."

"James was a weak man. He needed that. He needed to become someone else to reach his potential. Now he has. He's become Jack," Grant sneered.

"But Grant, everything you do is for yourself. You don't do anything that doesn't benefit you," I said. "Your friend and comrade was in jail for a murder you know he didn't commit. But it didn't benefit you or your business to get him out of it the right way. You could have turned in whoever did it and got him out. Instead, you hired us to prolong it, but we did what you couldn't. We stepped up."

Grant was getting agitated as he said, "I hired you because you couldn't even solve your own wife's murder. I hired you because I didn't think there was a chance in hell that you would get anywhere near the truth. You are insignificant—just ask around."

"Well, that may be true, Grant. And you're correct, I haven't been able to solve my wife's murder. But I have caught you. I have you involved in many ways with the murder of Helen Mazer. You may not have been the one to slit her throat, but you definitely killed her."

"I think we're done here, gentlemen," Grant said while standing up. His financial team was standing at the door.

"OK, Grant, we can be done for today. But know this isn't over," I said.

CHAPTER 50

WE THANKED JULIE BEFORE we left. We had to get to our next meeting. Lewis had set up another appointment for us. We couldn't trust the police because we knew Grant had gotten to at least Detective Tanner but couldn't be sure if anyone else was involved. Lewis had a contact, Grady Humble, in the New York City field office of the FBI.

We walked into Grady's office and went through the whole story. We showed him the video and let him know that we had just confronted Grant.

Grady said, "You probably shouldn't have done that. He's going to go into panic mode and start destroying any evidence. We need to move on this quickly, like right now. Let me make a quick call and get approval from my boss. With the police corruption involved, it shouldn't be an issue."

While Grady made a call to his boss, we waited outside. I was feeling anxious because I didn't want to let Grant slip through. When Grady came out to meet us, he said, "We're good to go. I want to get Jack and Grant into a room together. From what I've heard from you three, and what I saw, I think they're together on this. We should head straight to Dogon Tech. I have calls in for a warrant for Grant's car and office."

I said, "Great. We were leaning that way as well. We'll follow your lead."

■ ■ ■

When we arrived at Dogon Tech, we went straight in and passed through security. They tried to stop us, but Agent Humble and his partner, Agent Hicks, flashed their badges, and we kept walking. We took him to Grant's office. Grant and Jack were in there, with Grant shouting at Jack to grab things.

When we charged in, Grady announced himself, and they both stopped in shock. Grady said, "We need both of you to come down to our offices. You can either come in peace or we can have a team down here in two minutes swarming the building and take you in by force with a lot of television coverage."

Grant snapped out if it. "We'll come down. We have nothing to hide. Right, Jack?"

Jack looked scared but said, "Yeah, sure, whatever you say, Grant."

Grady got a phone call. When he finished talking, he shot us a look and asked, "Lewis, can you watch these two with Agent Hicks? I need to talk to Craig and Angelo outside the office really quick."

"Got it," Lewis said.

When we stepped out of the office, Grady said, "Craig, there's always video recording in that office, correct?"

"Yes."

"OK, Angelo, we have the warrant for the car. I want you to go back in there and see if you can get them talking. I'm going to check the car."

Craig and I walked back into Grant's office. Craig tapped me on the shoulder, so I let him take the lead. He knew these two better than I did. He strode over to sit down at Grant's desk. It was a power move and a smart move. He wanted to show Grant that he was in charge now, and Grant couldn't access the security system if Craig was there to stop him.

Craig asked, "So, Jack, is Grant going to let you take the fall for this too?"

Grants shot back, "Jack, don't say a word. They don't have anything."

Craig took another shot, working a different angle. "Jack, has Grant told you about Detective Tanner? He's got him under his thumb. Sound familiar?"

Jack started to talk but, after a glance at Grant, didn't say a word. Grant said, "He knows what he needs to know. But we don't need to discuss that here. Why are we still here? I want my lawyer, and Jack wants his as well."

I said, "Well, Grant, that FBI agent that was in here is down searching your car right now. He has a warrant and will soon have one for your office. How does that make you feel?"

"That can't be! What probable cause does he have to search my vehicle?"

Lewis decided he wanted in on the fun and explained, "Grant, we told you we knew about Detective Tanner, but we didn't say that he told us. You assumed that. We actually watched a video from this office from the night you made Detective Tanner come in. We saw the whole deal go down. And we watched you take your so-called evidence bag to your car in the garage. So, there's your probable cause—at least, that's how the FBI views it."

"But how? I deleted the security system that night! I mean... there was a glitch that evening."

I laughed a little before saying, "Ah, there it is. Don't worry, Grant. We know about that too. You've been deleting the security system on nights that you didn't like what went on in here. At first, it was only when Craig here would bring you inflated numbers, and you would feed him some story and make him fix them. But as you got deeper into this thing, you needed to cover more tracks, so you deleted that meeting with Tanner as well. But Cal left us a departing gift when he passed away. He overrode your system and kept a copy of the video feeds that you erased."

"I knew I had that prick killed for a reason!" Grant blurted out. I could see his wheels turning, realizing his mistake too late, trying to figure out a way out of that comment.

Craig yelled, "You had Cal killed and you killed my wife?!"

Grant had gained his composure. "I did not kill Cal, and I would never hurt your wife. I loved her."

Just then, Grady returned, holding up the bag we had seen in the video. "Then what are these bloody clothes doing in your car, Grant? Whose blood will we find on them?"

"No comment. I want my lawyer now, please."

CHAPTER 51

AFTER CRAIG DOWNLOADED THE video from the server, we all took a ride down to the FBI New York City field office. Grant and Jack were loaded into another vehicle with Agent Hicks, under arrest for the murder of Cal Dunst and under suspicion of being involved in the murder of Helen Mazer. The FBI also sent a car to pick up Detective Tanner.

On the ride back, Grady explained to Craig that he could no longer be a part of the investigation. He was too close to the situation and would be needed as a witness. He also needed Craig to talk about the relationships between himself, Grant, Jack, and Helen. Craig said he understood and would step back from being part of our investigative team.

Once we reached the offices, Grady wanted to interview Craig first. He wanted to get a sense of the whole picture since he had just gotten involved. Grant and Jack were put into separate interview rooms, awaiting questioning and their lawyers. We were also waiting for the DNA tests of the blood on the clothes found in Grant's car. Detective Tanner arrived and was placed in another interview room.

Craig and Grady were set up in an interview room. Lewis and I weren't allowed in the room, but they did allow us to watch through a video feed. Grady announced to the camera and Craig that this interview would be recorded. Craig and Grady went through Grant and Craig's relationship first. He told him all about the military, Jack's discharge, and all the companies that he had worked for Grant throughout their history.

Then Grady asked about Helen and Grant's relationship. Craig reported how long they had known each other, even before Craig had met Helen. Grady asked, "Were they ever involved romantically?"

Craig answered, "No, they never dated or were involved until recently. I found out that she had had an affair with him about six months ago. But we all worked through it; it was a one-time thing."

Lewis and I shared a look. Neither of us had heard about that before today.

"OK, Craig, what about you and Jack Gaither?"

"When we first met, he was James Grayson. We came up through basic training together. We were best friends. When Grant became our platoon leader, James and I sort of had a falling out, both trying to be second in command. It's been like that ever since, always vying for Grant's attention."

"Alright, Craig, that's all I have for now, but we need you to stay in here until after we've talked to Grant and Jack."

"Understood."

■ ■ ■

Everyone stayed and had to sleep in their interview rooms. Their lawyers had sat and waited for interrogations, only to be told that they would need to be back at six in the morning for the questions to begin. Lewis and I filled in any holes that Grady had questions on with the case. We stayed up throughout the night going over the case and awaiting the DNA results.

The next morning, the DNA results came back on the clothes. It was a match for Helen Mazer's blood. Grady headed straight to Grant Dogon's interview room. He was in there with his lawyer. Grady turned on the video feed and announced to the room that this interview would be recorded.

Grady started, "Grant Dogon, we have you on video admitting that you had Cal Dunst killed, we found bloody clothes in your car with Helen Mazer's blood, and we have video of you bribing a police officer. What do you have to say for yourself?"

The lawyer said, "We have no comment at this time."

Grady said, "That's fine. We have your buddy Jack next door, and he's told us all about it. How you hired someone to kill Cal. He said that you were never going to give Detective Tanner any evidence because it pointed to you and that you were going to blackmail him. He also told us that it wasn't just a one-time thing with Helen—the affair—that you had a long-standing relationship with her, and she was going to tell Craig, and that's why you killed her."

"I didn't kill Helen! I loved her! Those clothes in the car aren't mine; they're Jack's. He's the one who killed her! He confessed to me the night he did it!" Grant was shouting, while his lawyer was trying to get him to shut up.

"So, you aren't denying that you had Cal killed and bribed Detective Tanner?"

Grant had calmed down and said, "No comment."

"Well, while you think about it, I'm going to talk to Jack. How about you discuss with your lawyer the comments you need to be making."

Grady turned off the video feed. Seconds later, the video feed came back on. He had gone directly to Jack's room. Jack was also with his lawyer.

Grady began, "Just so you're aware, this interview will be recorded. Jack, Grant told me that the clothes we found in his car belong to you. It's still at the lab, but it had Helen Mazer's blood all over it. Are we going to find your DNA on it as well?"

Jack peered at his lawyer, and his lawyer said, "No comment."

Grady said, "OK, if that's how you're going to play this, I'll just come back when I get the DNA results from the clothing. Just know, Grant is over there telling me how much he loved Helen and how you killed her and confessed to him. I'll be back soon."

Grady turned off the video feed. He came into the room where Lewis and I had been watching. As he walked in, Grady asked, "What do you guys think? You've been involved for a lot longer than me."

"I think we need to wait for the rest of the DNA results before we make conclusions. Also, I think you need to keep Craig here. His answers were not what we expected," I said.

"What are you saying, Angelo? Aren't you two the ones who got him out of jail?" Grady asked, confused.

I said, "Look, I don't know yet, but I have a feeling that we need to keep Craig here."

"OK, Angelo. Lewis, you agree?"

"Sure do," Lewis said as he gave me the side-eye, wondering what I was thinking.

CHAPTER 52

WHILE WE WERE WAITING on the DNA results from the clothing, Grady interviewed Detective Tanner. Grady started like the other interviews by saying it would be recorded, but he also stated that Detective Tanner said he was willing to talk without a lawyer present.

Grady confirmed, "Is that correct, Detective Tanner, you're waiving your right to a lawyer?"

Detective Tanner simply said, "Yes."

Tanner broke quickly. He barely put up a fight, insisting that he only did it to solve the murder and get the credit. He figured it was only a few weeks, and if he could get some financial gain and solve the case that it would be OK in the end. He knew what he did was wrong and would accept whatever punishment would be given to him.

We heard from the lab, and they needed DNA from Craig, Grant, and Jack to determine whose DNA was on the clothing. So, Grady collected the samples and told everyone that they would be spending the night here again. No one declined to be swabbed. He sent the swabs to the lab. He told us to go home and get some rest. When the results come back tomorrow, he would let us know right away.

■ ■ ■

Lewis and I were exhausted. We headed to his place to get some dinner and rest up for the next day. Lewis asked me when we got to his penthouse, "What was all that about Craig back there? I know I agreed with you, but it's because I know you, and you must have something. So, what is it?"

"I'm not a hundred percent sure yet, Lewis. But when Craig said that Grant and Helen had had an affair six months ago, he hadn't mentioned that to us. Also, he said that he and Jack were close—another thing he failed to tell us. If Craig really had wanted to help us, these things would have been of great importance when he told us about their relationships with him. I just feel like there's more going on, like when we first got involved. Something isn't right."

"OK, I hear you, but like Grady said, we helped get him out of this mess. And we believed in him. Vanesa believed him. So, I'm not saying you're wrong here, but what has you going against your instincts?"

"My instincts, again. Like I said, I'm not sure, but I don't want to rule anything out. He held out on us, and we need to know why."

CHAPTER 53

WE SHOWED UP AT the FBI field office early the next morning. Grady strolled into the video room and said, "It's Jack's DNA on the clothing. Looks like Grant was telling the truth about that part. We have our killer. We will be charging Jack Gaither, aka James Grayson, with the murder of Helen Mazer. Grant Dogon will be charged with murder for hire in the killing of Cal Dunst; he will also be charged with bribing a public official, tampering of evidence, and obstruction of justice. And finally, Detective Tanner will be charged with accepting a bribe as a public official and with tampering of evidence. You guys did great work, and I appreciate you bringing it to me. It'll look good for the FBI on this one. But, before you go, we'll be doing one more video feed while Jack and Grant are being placed under arrest. And hopefully while that happens, one or both will get talkative. Do you want to stay and watch?"

"Yes, I'd like to see their faces when they get arrested," I replied.

As Grady left our room, he was joined by a fellow agent, and they walked into Grant's room. The video feed turned on. Grady began by reading him his rights then stating all the charges against him. They put him in handcuffs and took him out. Grant didn't say a word. The video feed cut out. Grady passed by our room with Grant in handcuffs. He stopped to says he would be right back to arrest Jack.

Grady returned with the other agent, and they went into Jack's room. The video feed turned on. He followed the same routine with Jack, but Jack shook his head vehemently. He shouted, "No! I am not going down alone for this! Not this time! I want to talk! Let's talk."

Jack's lawyer was aggressively telling him to shut up and to just go with the agents. But Jack said, "No! You're fired, and I do not require an attorney present for what I'm about to say. I waive my right."

The lawyer sat there, dumbstruck by what he was witnessing, until Grady said, "You heard the man—leave."

CHAPTER 54

ONCE THE COMMOTION WAS over and the lawyer had packed up his things and left, Grady and the other agent took a seat across from Jack. Grady studied Jack and said, "OK, Jack, I'm listening, but we have your clothing with Helen Mazer's blood all over them. What else could you have to say?"

Jack was tearing up as he started to talk, "Look, I admit it. I killed Helen Mazer. Now you have your confession. But there's more to it than that. I'm not the only one involved, and I'm not going to take all the blame alone like before. This whole plan was Craig's idea."

Lewis looked at me, and while I was as shocked as he was, I knew there was more to the story. Grady said, "You expect me to believe that Craig knew you were sleeping with his wife and knew you were going to kill her?"

"Craig started planning this back when he found out that Helen had had an affair with Grant. He told me that he could never look at either of them the same way anymore. He wanted to ruin both of their lives and take over Dogon Tech by setting up Grant. He came to me for help. He knew that I had harbored some hatred for Grant because he always treated me like he was doing me a favor, when in actuality, I had saved his life when I took the fall in the military. He owed me, and I figured by helping Craig, I would finally get my payback."

Grady interjected, "But Grant paid you both well, right? You guys have some serious cash because of Grant Dogon."

"It wasn't about the money; it's about respect. Grant walked all over both of us, and when he had the affair with Helen, Craig broke.

"About a month after he found out about the affair, Craig started telling me he wanted revenge, but I thought he was just blowing off steam. I had heard that the three of them made up. But then he approached me with a crazy request. He said that he wanted me to seduce his wife and start another affair. I asked him what that would solve, and he said that he wanted her to fall for me and then we would kill her and set up Grant. Grant would go away for murder, and Craig would take over the company and the public sale.

"I was supposed to kill her twice before the night of her death, but I couldn't do it. I had fallen in love with her. Then it happened. She told me she was ending it and telling Craig all about our affair. I lost it, and things spun out of control. I smashed a mug in the fire and ran into the kitchen to think. I called Craig while I was in the kitchen after she told me. He said to do it right then. Kill her, and the company would be ours. I was out of my mind, and I started breaking things in the kitchen. Then she came in, and I decided that no one could be with her but me. That's when I grabbed the knife… Well, you know the rest."

Grady was, like Lewis and me, speechless. Eventually he looked up and said, "That's an awful story, Jack. How can we know that you're not just throwing Craig under the bus because you got caught?"

Jack was crying. He said, "Check my phone records. You'll see that I called Craig that night. Also, there are voice mails from Craig asking me if it was done yet on the two previous times he had wanted me to kill her."

"OK, say we confirm all of that. Why did you go to Dogon Tech in your bloody clothes?"

"It was the final part of Craig's plan. He knew Grant would help me but also hold it over my head. He knew that if I wore the clothes there, Grant would keep them in case I decided to cross him. That part worked; he kept them, and you originally thought they were his. Obviously, we didn't think about you not assuming they were his."

Jack stood up, defeated and exhausted, and said, "I'm done. Let's go."

CHAPTER 55

AFTER WALKING OUT JACK, Grady came in to talk to us. "Well, that went a lot differently than I thought it would. Looks like we have another arrest to make."

"Grady, can we participate in this one? I'd like to talk to Craig as well. We have some things we'd like to know."

"It's against protocol, but you helped solve this whole thing by pursuing the shutdowns at Dogon Tech, so it's the least I can do."

We all entered Craig's room. Grady turned on the video feed to record. Craig said, "Hey, guys, what's going on? I've been sitting here for two days. Did they arrest Grant yet?"

Before he could say anything else, Grady read him his rights and told him he was being charged with the murder of Helen Mazer.

He just stared at all three of us, but he didn't look surprised or shocked. He looked relieved. He stood up and said, "I'm sorry, Angelo and Lewis. You didn't deserve to be dragged through this whole mess. Let's go, Agent Humble."

He held out his hands for the handcuffs to be put on, and Grady walked him out.

CHAPTER 56

ONE MONTH LATER

Craig, Grant, and Jack had all been formally charged at their arraignments and were awaiting trial. I don't think any of them will beat the charges, but I've seen stranger things. The trials seemed to be more of a formality to see how long each of their sentences would be. Detective Tanner was sentenced to 5 years in prison for a class 2 felony for accepting a bribe. I think if he had accepted the shares and a transaction was made, then he would have gotten longer, but he had never received anything.

They had finally released Helen Mazer's body for a proper burial, and Lewis offered to pay for a funeral and plot. No matter what her sins were, she did not deserve to be killed and she deserved a funeral. I had to go the police station to formally release the body to the funeral home, as Craig had requested that I do it. I hadn't seen Craig since that day in the FBI office, but he did call me once to ask me for this favor. I asked him to sit down and talk to me, and then I would carry out this for him. So, on the way to sign the release, I stopped by the prison.

I knew the routine well as I turned over my belongings to the clerk. They took me back to the open visiting area.

Out walked Grant Dogon, in a much less expensive jumpsuit, but even orange looked good on him. His hair was still perfect. I decided I would only make this visit once, so I figured I'd talk to both Grant and Craig today.

When Grant reached the table, he didn't immediately sit down; instead, he asked gruffly, "What do you want, Angelo?"

"Grant, please sit. This isn't a hostile visit. I just wanted to talk to you. Please?"

Grant sat down, but on the edge of his seat, like he was ready to get up at a moment's notice. He said, "Fine, but I don't have much to say to you. You ruined my life and my accomplishments."

"Well, Grant, I think you have yourself to blame for those. Had you only turned in Jack when he came to you, you wouldn't have ever been involved. All of these charges you were convicted for happened after that moment you made the decision to protect Jack."

Grant cast his eyes down and shook his head. Then he sat back in his chair, getting comfortable. When he met my gaze, he said, "I was doing what I was taught: protect and lead. These were my men. What else was I supposed to do?"

"Grant, that was the military, and this is the real world. The rules of engagement are different here. You should have done the right thing and honored your friend Helen, someone you knew longer than either Craig or Jack."

"Did you just come here to lecture me?"

"No, Grant, I wanted to see you accept responsibility for your part in this. You would have changed three lives if you did the right thing instead of trying to protect those who did wrong. And they ended up going down for it anyways and managed to take you with them. But no, I'm not here to lecture you. I want you to always remember Cal Dunst, Detective Tanner, and yourself. Your choices affected each of them in the worst way possible. Just remember that."

I called the guards over and told them I was done with Grant. They took Grant back to his cell. I sat and waited, satisfied with my conversation with Grant.

When Craig came out, he was in handcuffs and leg chains. He sat down across from me. This time he looked more hardened than my previous visits when he was pretending to mourn his wife's death.

He started by saying, "Thank you for taking care of Helen's funeral service and burial. I'm sure you don't think I care, but I do."

"I'm not doing it for you, Craig, I'm doing it for her."

"OK, I understand, but thanks all the same."

"Craig, what were you thinking? Once Jack killed her, did you really think you could pin it all on Grant and you would go on to run the company? Did you think Jack wouldn't have gotten caught either?"

"Angelo, I wasn't thinking. I was filled with a rage inside of me. I tried very hard to move past it, thinking it was a drunken mistake that Grant and Helen had made. But it wasn't. They both consciously turned off any feelings they had for me and acted on their lust. From that moment on, my only motivation to go on was revenge. And I acted on it. At the end of the day, I don't know that I would have done anything differently. Not because I wouldn't have wanted to, because I did, but because I don't think what's inside me would allow me to act any differently. Many people would say that I could've just gotten a divorce or quit my job or both. But why should I have to give up everything because of what others had done to me?

That's the real mystery here, Angelo. Why am I the one who was supposed to move on and pretend it was OK when I did nothing wrong?

"Did I think I'd get away with it? Maybe. Did I think I could pin it all on Grant? It could've happened. And did I think Jack would just be a puppet? Of course. And when he fell in love with her, I didn't care what happened to him. In the end, I didn't really care what happened to me. I got my revenge, and I have to live with it. When Grady read me my rights and charged me, I was able to breathe. For the first time in six months, I was able to just be. No more hiding, no more secrets, and no more regret.

"So, Angelo, did you get what you came for?"

I regarded him with more pity than I had at any time before and said, "Yeah, I think so. I wanted to hear why you did it and see if you had any remorse. I can see your point of view, but I don't agree with it. I did have one more question, though. Why not just say Grant killed your wife from the beginning? When we first were questioning you, it was like you were protecting him."

"You see, Angelo, I didn't just want Grant to go to jail. I wanted him to suffer. He had so much going on with the public sale and trying to protect the business that he was going crazy with all of this on top of it. I wanted to stretch out his agony for as long as possible. I wish that it didn't go as far as Cal getting killed, but there's always some collateral damage in war."

On that note, I stood up and walked out. I didn't want to give him any validation to what he had just said. Collateral damage was always wrong, and this wasn't a war.

■ ■ ■

Helen's funeral was the next day. I had signed the release, and they said they would send the body to the funeral home by the end of the day. We had invited the Rathmores, the Bayners, and the Hotches. They said they would take care of getting Helen's family there. There would be a service and then a memorial at the burial site.

CHAPTER 57

ON THE MORNING OF the funeral, I had a lot running through my mind. Funerals always make me think of Lucy and how she left me too soon. That led me to think of Vanesa and what she knew about my wife's murder and who she was running from.

I hadn't heard from Vanesa in a couple of weeks. The last thing she told me was that she was on the move again but thought she could come home soon. She said that she would tell me everything but only in person. Lewis assured me that she was safe.

Lewis came in his limousine to pick me up. We were heading to the funeral home early to make sure everything was set up in an honorable way for Helen's family and friends to remember her and her life. And hopefully, they would gain some closure almost two months after she was killed.

When the service started, the room was filled to capacity. There were family and friends, of course, but also Helen's Instagram followers and those weird people who simply wanted to be a part of this macabre mess Craig Mazer had created. The service was to be short, giving people the chance to say goodbye.

The memorial at the burial site was much more intimate—just family and close friends along with me and Lewis. There were many eulogies, with almost everyone there getting up to say something about Helen. It was the ending she deserved, especially after being taken from this world before her time.

We stood at the back of the burial site to allow the family their privacy while they said their final goodbyes. As each one left, though, they stopped by to thank us for this funeral and for giving Helen justice.

As the group lining up to thank us began to thin out, I noticed someone hanging at the back of the line. At first, I thought my mind was playing tricks on me, but no, it was Vanesa. I wanted to run to her, for fear she may leave again, but I remained standing there to be courteous to the people who wished to talk to us.

Finally, it was only Vanesa, Lewis, and me. But when I turned to gauge Lewis's reaction, he was gone as well. Vanesa walked up to me and said, "We need to talk…"

To be continued…

ACKNOWLEDGMENTS

I FIRST WANT TO thank my wife, Dawn, because without her, this wouldn't have been possible. Next, I want to thank my kids for their belief in me. Then I want to thank my mother and father for always pushing me to be my best. And lastly, I'd like to thank all the people who helped me get this book to the level that I wanted it to be: Milade Rasooli, Karen L. Tucker, Beth Lamkemeyer, Haider Aldugum, Everett Sherrod, Nick Atkinson, The Book Club (Kathy, Vickie, Theresa, Mary, Shari, and Beth), the Lava Lounge crew, Joni Erickson, and Karen Moore.

ABOUT THE AUTHOR

RYAN SPELL IS FROM St. Louis, Mo., where he still resides. He is an environmental consultant by trade but has always read great fiction books. He decided long ago to write his own, and he finally did. *An Army of Lies* is his first book. Ryan has a wife and two children, both boys.

FROM THE AUTHOR

THANK YOU FOR READING *An Army of Lies*. If you enjoyed this book (or even if you didn't), please visit the site where you purchased it and write a brief review. Your feedback is important to me and will help other readers decide whether to read the book, too. I hope if anything else, you will continue reading books, from me or any other author. Writing should inspire reading.

If you'd like to get notifications of new releases and special offers on my books, please join my email list by signing up on my website, www.ryanspell.com.

Ryan Spell, 2023

Printed in the USA
CPSIA information can be obtained
at www.ICGtesting.com
CBHW051517081223
2389CB00003BB/5